Joan Spence is 75 years of age and has two daughters and four grandchildren. She has been retired since 15 years from Hartlepool Bough Council, where she worked as a principal practitioner for children's services.

To my dear husband, who sadly passed away three years ago, for his assistance in reading through my proofs.

Joan Spence

EXIT TO ANOTHER DIMENSION

AUSTIN MACAULEY PUBLISHERS™

LONDON • CAMBRIDGE • NEW YORK • SHARJAH

A CIP catalogue record for this title is available from the British Library.

ISBN 9781398495289 (Paperback)
ISBN 9781398495296 (ePub e-book)

www.austinmacauley.com

First Published 2023
Austin Macauley Publishers Ltd®
1 Canada Square
Canary Wharf
London
E14 5AA

My husband and daughters encouraged me to write this book after I retired as it is always something I wanted to do. They helped me with reading through drafts and I thank my dear husband, who passed away three years ago, for a relentless reading of my drafts.

Chapter 1
Mysterious Sightings

It was mid-August and the hills above Keswick were as hot as Spain. Alex lifted his head from the mystery novel he was reading, pushed his glasses up his nose, and peered down the lane to see if Tom was on his way. Tom was Alex's best friend, and the pair of them were about to spend the night camping in the back garden.

Alex's mum had made pizza for tea, and they had a feast of biscuits, crisps and pop planned for later. The hay was in, the grain silo was full, and Alex's chores were all done for the day. In a few days, the straw stubble would need burning off, and the pasture would be ploughed, but for now, he could relax. He smiled to himself. His hand crept down to his pocket as he felt for his brand-new sheath knife. The dark wooden handle was smooth, with a rounded metal top. The shiny blade came to a sharp point and was protected by a thick leather holster. He'd promised his dad that he would keep it in the house, or just use it on the farm, but he couldn't resist showing it to his closest friend.

Alex was nearly 11. He had helped on Rook Farm – where he'd been born and raised – ever since he could walk. As a result of all that outdoor work, Alex was quite strong, although he was small in stature and his brown hair had been bleached by the sun.

The family bred sheep and cows and grew various crops in rotation. He knew just about all there was to know about running a farm, even though his head was in the clouds, sometimes.

Tom was taller than Alex, with long legs, piercing blue eyes and a shock of blonde hair. He also had a wry sense of humour. Both Tom and Alex were soon to be starting 'big' school, and there was a lot to talk about. Their other friend, Ben, who lived on another nearby farm wouldn't be joining them until the next night. He was stuck at home because it was his little brother, Charlie's, fifth birthday party. For now, though, it would be just the two of them. The boys had other friends from school, some of them living on farms as they did, but Tom was Alex's very best friend.

Alex adored living on the farm and spending time in the vast open spaces of the Lake District. They had acres of land stretching out from the farmhouse and he could ride his bike for miles in the lanes around their home. Alex did have to help his dad but he never minded. In fact, he enjoyed working in the fields. In particular, he loved working with the sheep. He and their border collie, Bess, would work together when they needed to be rounded up. She did most of the running, though. Alex would help to muck out the sheds and often sat on the tractor with his dad when he worked in the fields. They also had a couple of house cats, Mitzy and Sooty, who kept the mice and rats away. Bess doted on them and they would often play together. The cats would roll on their backs, wait for her to come near them, grab her legs with their paws, and she would bark at them. Their favourite game was chasing a scrunched-up crisp packet around the kitchen. Bess often went crashing into the table legs as she skidded across the floor. It went without saying that she would be keeping the boy's company for at least part of the night.

Tom lived on the next farm and as it was the summer holidays, they were spending a lot of time together once their jobs were done. They often slept outside in the large garden at the back of the house, and that night, hot as it was, would be no exception. The garden had a neat lawn with small borders around the edges filled with all kinds of colourful flowers. It was enclosed by a fence, with a creaky gate at the bottom which opened onto the lane. Beyond that were the fields.

That night, Alex and Tom had stayed up really late, giggling about nothing very much, and gorging themselves on their midnight feast. They eventually settled down after a telling-off from Alex's mother, who sent Bess back into her kennel. Alex wasn't the least bit tired so when Tom had fallen asleep, he had used his torch to read the next chapter of his book before finally closing his eyes. Then he nodded off, the book still in his hands, the torch making a broad yellow circle on the roof of the tent.

It was still dark when he woke with a start, heart thumping. He was sure he'd just heard the gate closing. It wasn't Tom – he was still there, fast asleep. There was no sign of Bess. Alex swiftly slithered over and peered out of the tent flap, his rapid breathing causing pain in his chest. He could just make out a figure moving away down the lane. Without a second thought, he grabbed the falling torch, crept out of the tent and ran towards the 'whatever-it-was. Without his glasses, though, all he could make out was a brown blur. It was in the pasture now and lumbering across the grass before abruptly disappearing from view. He stood stock still. He couldn't imagine who or what would be wandering about in the dark, miles from anywhere. He couldn't understand where Bess had disappeared to and why she hadn't barked to alert them – strange.

Now Alex's imagination was working overtime. He hadn't heard of any tales of strange animals in the area, except for big cats – and this was the wrong shape entirely. What or who could disappear that fast, or had he just imagined it? Without his glasses, and in the half-light, his eyes may have played tricks on him but no, he was sure he'd seen something move – something human or…

He shook himself, stumbled back into the tent and shook his friend to wake him.

'Tom, wake up!'

Tom rubbed his eyes and sat up, his fringe flopping in his face.

'What is it?' he muttered sleepily.

'I've just seen something going out through the gate. Something's been in the garden.'

'You've probably been dreaming. Go back to sleep Alex,' he mumbled, lying back down and turning away.

'No! It wasn't a dream! Something was here. It gave me a start, but when I got up to look, it just disappeared.'

Tom didn't answer. He'd already drifted back to sleep, but Alex couldn't settle. Someone or something had been in the garden. He definitely hadn't imagined it.

Later, at breakfast, Tom told Alex's parents all about his 'dream' making a huge joke of it. Alex was furious, especially when his mother responded as she usually did – reminding them of all of his over-active imagination. She raised her eyebrows, tucked in her chin and frowned at him. Alex scowled angrily at them all. Tom wouldn't like Alex making fun of him. He'd probably have punched him and gone off in a huff. Bess, who was under the table, put a sympathetic paw on his knee. Alex stroked her absent-mindedly. He was thinking. He vowed to be more vigilant that night. He'd keep his glasses handy – even sleep with them on – keep the torch in his hand…and perhaps with Ben's help, who would be with them that night, he would show them it wasn't a dream.

Alex didn't like anyone laughing at him, not least his best friend. He was quite used to his mother's attitude, but it didn't hurt any less. She would dismiss what he said as fantasies, half the time. However, whatever he'd seen the night before was definitely real. Alex was determined 'it' wouldn't escape this time, if it came back, and then they would have to believe him. They would haveto!

That night, it was just Alex and Tom again. Ben hadn't shown up, but they weren't worried – his father had probably found him something else to do, they thought. Alex fell asleep despite his best efforts to keep awake but a noise woke him just as it was starting to get light. He shot out of the tent, yelling, 'Tom, come quickly now!'

Tom rubbed his eyes, but this time, instead of rolling over and going back to sleep, he stumbled out of the tent and rambled over towards the gate. He was muttering under his breath and glared at Alex, annoyed at being woken up again.

'What?' he said, sighing.

'In the distance, you can just see…'

'No! You can't see anything. You've had that dream again,' he said crossly.

Alex was livid that Tom hadn't seen anything but he couldn't argue. Tom was right. There was nothing there. It had vanished again as suddenly as before.

'I'm going over there to have a look. It can't have disappeared that quickly. Maybe there's a hole,' he suggested, as he strode towards the spot where he'd seen 'it' disappear.

Alex wasn't looking at Tom or listening to his groaning about being woken at an unearthly hour. Tom was shaking his head but he still followed his friend. He wanted to prove that it was all in Alex's imagination.

Perhaps he would shut up about it then. Alex did go on sometimes.

When they reached the place where he had last seen the 'being' Alex stood scratching his head. There was no sign that anything had ever been there. He couldn't understand it. He was sure it wasn't his imagination because twice he'd seen 'it' and twice it had suddenly vanished.

'Aw come on, Alex, admit it. It was just a dream,' Tom said, rolling his eyes in exasperation.

Tom knew Alex could get carried away if he thought there was a mystery to solve. It was those books he read. Alright, they were fiction but Alex believed the stories could be based on reality.

'I've told you it wasn't a dream. Why can't you believe me?' he said through gritted teeth, his face flushing bright red.

Alex dropped to his hands and knees and scrambled about the ground feeling for some kind of hole. He was breathing heavily as he searched frantically for something that would convince Tom that he was right. He was becoming desperate. He had to find something, anything, to show that it wasn't his imagination this time.

'I know it was here, it can't have just disappeared,' he said, frowning as he continued to probe the ground.

Tom had started to walk away from him, back towards the garden.

'You're being really…' but Tom's voice had faded away. Alex heard a faint whooshing sound behind him and spun around to see what it was. Tom wasn't there! He'd gone! It took a moment for the fact to register …

'Tom! Tom! Where are you?' he screamed. 'Stop playing about, it's just not funny!'

In a blind panic, Alex crawled around on his hand and knees searching the ground for some kind of a hole. Tom must be somewhere! He couldn't just disappear!

Maybe the whooshing sound was Tom being sucked down into the ground, he thought. Alex remained motionless for some time, listening hard. He felt sick with fright, his stomach churning. Where was his friend? He wished they hadn't come into the pasture. He continued to search like a person possessed. His whole body was tense and he felt unable to breathe. Maybe there was a pothole he didn't know about.

After some time, and feeling very frustrated and frightened, Alex ran, as fast as his legs would go, back to the farmhouse. Shaking, he fell through the kitchen door. His mother was standing by the sink looking out the window, a mug of tea in her hand.

'Mum, Tom's disappeared!' he shouted, his voice high and tight.

Startled, she spun around, and dropped the mug she was holding. It showered the cupboard doors with tea, the rest leaving a puddle on the floor amongst the broken bits of porcelain. The cats, who had been dozing in Bess's bed, now stood bristling in the corner by the door.

'What on earth…' she managed to say, lifting her hands in astonishment, before Alex yelled again. 'Didn't she hear what he had said?'

'He's disappeared from the pasture!'

'What do you mean, he's disappeared? Did he just go home? He's probably playing a trick on you'.

Exasperated, Alex hardly paused for breath before launching into his story.

'I saw that" thing" again. It ran across the pasture and then disappeared. Tom and I went to have a look and we were talking and then I heard a noise. When I turned around, he had gone, Mum. I think he's been sucked into the ground but I couldn't find a hole anywhere.' He gasped for air as he finished, flushed and panting as if he'd just run a marathon.

'Oh, don't be silly, Alex, people don't just suddenly disappear. He's probably got tired of your stories and decided to go home.'

Alex was so astounded he couldn't speak. Why couldn't his mum believe him? His best friend had vanished only metres away from him and she was dismissing this tragedy as if it were something he had made up. He shook with rage. Seeing his distress, she sighed and gave him a despairing look.

'I'll phone his mum,' she said, 'he's probably home by now.'

'He won't be at home,' Alex yelled at her. 'He's gone!' His mother, however, was not listening to him, she'd picked up the phone.

Whilst waiting for an answer she mouthed at Alex to clear up the broken china from the floor.

'Oh, hello Angela. Um, is Tom home yet?'

'No. I thought he was still with you. Isn't he?'

'No…he and Alex have had some sort of disagreement, I think, and he's left for home.'

'Well, he hasn't arrived yet. I suppose he'll be here any minute. I'll let you know when he gets in.'

Alex sat with his head in his hands, the crockery untouched. Had Tom gone home while he was searching the ground in the pasture? Yes, he'd had his back to Tom, but surely, he would have seen him as soon as he turned around. After all, there was nowhere to hide up there. No, Alex had heard Tom's voice fading out, along with the whooshing noise seconds later, and then nothing. He must have been taken by that 'thing'. There was no other explanation. He sat staring at his mum and shaking his head – parents, why don't they ever believe what you say!

Chapter 2
Camping Out

Tom's parents came up to Rook farm when he didn't arrive home.

Alex sat with his head bowed. He'd told his mum what had happened and now they were all looking at him as if he'd gone stark raving mad. *Typical*, he thought. Now they were asking him to repeat his story, pushing him to tell the truth. Tell them what had really happened, while they tried to make some sense of it.

Alex's mind was in a whirl. Adults were supposed to have the answer to everything. They were supposed to make things right, and here they were quizzing him about what had happened, asking him for the truth.

He'd told them the truth, why couldn't they understand that? He looked up. They were all staring at him, his dad wore a puzzled frown. He moved towards Alex and placed a hand on his shoulder.

'Alright, son, just tell me exactly what you saw, and what happened before Tom disappeared,' said his dad in a calm voice. He still looked as though he didn't believe a word of Alex's story.

'I've told you what I saw. It was something…something brown…the shape of a human or whatever dressed in brown. It vanished! Then I was on my hands and knees searching the grass for a hole. I had my back to Tom and he started to say something, and then I heard this whooshing noise. When I turned around, he'd gone.'

He glared at his dad, why did he have to keep repeating his story? What was it they didn't understand? His best friend had gone and here they were standing around asking him questions instead of trying to find him.

It was his mum who finally suggested they should contact the police. Alex couldn't think what they'd be able to do. Mountain rescue might be more appropriate. But he kept those thoughts to himself.

After what seemed like an age, but was probably only about 20 minutes, two uniformed officers arrived at the house. Alex went through his short, but apparently unbelievable story, yet again. He looked in frustration at the officers and his parents. Why couldn't they just believe what he was saying and do something about it? This was his best friend they were talking about and something had to be done, he was worried sick. Talking wouldn't find him. His dad was looking at him sympathetically.

'Take us to the spot where you and Tom were, son.' *At last*, thought Alex, *someone believes me*. They all trooped out of the back door, except Bess who, for once, seemed quite happy to stay in the house. They went through the garden and across the lane to the pasture, to the area where he had been searching.

'This is it. Look.' Alex swept his arm around. 'It's just open pasture. If Tom had just walked off, I would have seen him.'

He stood watching them all shaking their heads, waiting for someone to say something. Tom's mum had started to cry quietly, and her husband put a comforting arm around her. Alex felt sick.

The police spent some time searching the pasture but, of course, found nothing. One of the officers suggested that perhaps a poacher may have been digging deep pits to trap animals, and Tom had fallen into one and banged his head. There was an awful lot of pasture to cover and they had probably just missed the spot where he had fallen. Alex was shaking his head; he'd heard Tom's voice fading away before he disappeared…he can't have been that far away from him.

The police left sometime later after going over every part of the pasture, saying they would call mountain rescue just in case, and do some house-to-house calls.

That afternoon, Alex opened the door to one of the police officers. He had hoped there was news of Tom, but no, this was worse. Ben Johnson had also disappeared from the next farm.

Apparently, he'd been amusing his little brother, Charlie, playing with the border collies, and Charlie had come in crying saying that Ben had left him, the officer told them.

'His parents have searched the surroundings and outbuildings and there is no sign of him. All little Charlie could say was that he was there and then he disappeared. He hasn't stopped crying since.'

Chasing his food around his plate that evening, Alex couldn't stop thinking about Tom and Ben. His head was down and he stared, trance-like, at his meal. He couldn't think straight.

'Not hungry, son?' his dad asked. Hungry? Alex felt positively sick with worry.

'No, not really,' he replied to his throat tight. He didn't want to talk. He wanted to be out looking for his friends. After a moment or so he put his knife and fork down and looked at his dad.

'Dad let's camp out in the pasture tonight. If we stay awake, we might see what came into the garden. Perhaps we could find Tom and Ben. Maybe they've been taken to another world underneath our pasture.'

His dad sighed.

'You've been reading too much science fiction, son. Things don't happen like that in real life. There are no underground worlds and people don't just disappear like that,' he said stroking the side of Alex's head.

'Yes, they do. Tom and Ben have both disappeared. Anyway, what about the Bermuda triangle? People have been beamed up by aliens before,' he protested. Mum interrupted their conversation.

'You are certainly not camping out overnight in any pasture and that's the end of this conversation.'

'Oh, Mum. Nothing's going to happen to us. Surely you want to find out who has taken Tom and Ben. I'll be safe with Dad honestly.'

'Something is going on that we can't explain at the minute and until the police have found your friends, I want you right where I can see you,' she said in a voice that brooked no argument on the matter. There was a lengthy pause…

'Don't I get a say in all of this, you two?' asked his dad.

'No, you don't, Dan,' she answered glaring at him. 'I said you are not sleeping in the pasture. No way…'

'Please Dad, it's worth a try.' Alex stared at his dad, his eyes unwavering, begging him to agree with him.

'Julie, the lad's right. No harm is going to come to us if we stay in the pasture overnight. I'll be there and so will Bess. We'll camp as close to the house as we can, it's worth a go. The police haven't found anything yet. I will stay awake, I promise you,' he said winking at her and offering silent assurances that if it would keep Alex happy it would be worth it.

'I have told you both!' she snapped. 'I'm not going to say it anymore. You are not camping out there tonight!' By now she was looking angrily at both of them but deep down knew that she was outnumbered. Soon afterwards, Alex and his dad were busy moving the tent from the garden to the pasture across the lane.

Alex was secretly pleased that his dad had won the argument. He usually did, in the end. He wasn't so sure about Bess staying with them, though. Normally she didn't like to miss anything and would stick to Alex like glue when they were together, but she must have slunk off as soon as she'd sensed the 'thing' because he hadn't seen her around when it was there.

That night as the sun was setting, Alex and his dad went out to the tent. They were closely followed by Bess, who seemed more subdued than normal.

They had brought food and something to drink, as well as a flask of strong coffee to keep his dad awake. Alex had brought his knife with him. He could use this to protect them.

Then the 'whatever-it-was' would be scared and let Tom and Ben go. That's what he hoped, anyway.

'Right son. You go to sleep when you're ready. I'll keep watch,' his dad promised. Alex didn't really want to go to sleep, so he read some more of his book but after a while, his eyes began to feel heavy and he fell into a deep slumber, dreaming of aliens, invisible spaceships and weird disappearances into an underground world. It was still dark when he woke with a start. Something sharp had pricked his arm, making him jump. At first, he thought he was still dreaming. It felt as though he was floating out of the tent but then he realised that he was being carried along in the arms of a big man – well he assumed it was a man. Alex turned his head. He, or whoever it was, had a coat on and his head was covered by a hood which seemed to hide his face.

'Dad!' he yelled, but no sound came out of his mouth. It was like one of those terrifying dreams when you open your mouth and no noise comes out. Alex twisted pushed and struggled to try and get free, but whatever had a hold of him had a vice-like grip. He hit out hard at its chest, but it was like thumping a brick wall. What was it? It didn't even flinch when Alex punched it and he knew he could hit really hard. All he'd done was hurt his own knuckles and now he was really terrified.

He craned his head to try and get a glimpse of the tent. His dad was scrambling through the flap, looking around wildly and rubbing his eyes. He could see Bess only a few metres away. She looked as if she was barking furiously but he couldn't hear anything – he had gone deaf.

He felt himself rising, in the arms of 'it', and his dad raising his arms but he couldn't reach him. His dad was yelling, he could see his mouth moving but there was no sound and his own attempts to cry out had no effect, he couldn't hear his own voice. Then...they were inside some kind of metal room and he was being strapped to a cold, shiny wall. Alex started to feel drowsy and could hardly keep his eyes open. He tried to focus on his captor whose hooded face he still couldn't see, clearly. There was another similar figure on the other side of the room. It had its back to him and was fiddling with some controls and monitors. Alex had to squint to see, but the equipment looked like something out of a plane cockpit.

'Where am I...and who the heck are you?' Alex yelled furiously but still; no sound came out of his mouth. Why couldn't he speak? Okay, Alex decided that even if he couldn't shout, he was determined to overcome these beings and escape. They were staring at him silently. Alex struggled to undo the strap that was holding him but as he did so he felt his legs turn to jelly. His attempts to vent his rage were futile as energy seemed to drain from his body There was a very loud whooshing noise and some coloured sparks, and he made one more attempt to shout for his dad which was futile. That was his last thought before he passed out.

When he woke again, he sat up slowly and looked around. He tried hard to recall what had happened – he remembered the machine and his useless efforts to scream, and then there was nothing. His head felt fuzzy and it ached. Alex struggled to focus his eyes, but everything seemed blurred. He was in a bed but not in his bedroom. Where was he? Alex could just about make out a pale square, which he guessed must be a window. He rubbed his eyes and looked at his watch. It was seven o'clock, and yet it seemed as though it was only just becoming light. *Not right for summer*, he thought. Perhaps his watch was wrong, he shivered. Alex blinked a few times, and as he did, his vision slowly began to clear. He could see that he was in a large room with half a dozen beds in, and there appeared to be someone sleeping in two of the furthest ones from him. He eased himself gingerly out of the bed and crept over to the sleeping figures. As he approached, one of them murmured something and turned towards him. It was Tom! Alex was so relieved he felt like hugging him but this wouldn't be a 'cool' thing to do with his friend, he would probably slog him one. Instead, he shook him gently.

'Tom,' he whispered, 'it's me, Alex. Wake up!'

Tom opened his eyes and stared at him for a moment or two, then a look of relief spread over his face.

'Alex! I'm not dreaming, am I? It is you?'

'Yes, of course, it's me. Crumbs, I'm so pleased to see you. I thought you'd gone forever.'

'Alex, I'm so sorry I made fun of you, you were right and I didn't believe what you saw. I feel such a jerk,' he whispered.

There was a noise from the next bed and they both turned to look in that direction.

'Alex!' exclaimed Ben, as he started to sit up. 'It's so good to see you, but do you know where we are?'

Ben was very much like Alex in appearance, except his hair was darker, as were his eyes. The three of them shuffled over to the window. The room they were in was pretty high up, at least three floors they ascertained.

As they peered down, they could just make out blurred figures. All wore brown trousers and brown hooded jackets. There were about half a dozen of them and they were working on the land below them. They appeared to be digging and putting something into large baskets. The plant life didn't look any different, certainly not other-worldly. Alex was convinced now, that it hadn't been a dream. He thought of himself as quite tough and although he wasn't frightened, he did wish that he'd listened to his mum and stayed inside the house…but then again, he wouldn't have found his friends.

Alex was feeling a mixture of tension and excitement. He knew all about shapeshifting. There were tales of aliens living on other planets but he never dreamed he would actually meet one – never mind a few of them.

Ben disturbed his thoughts. 'If they are aliens, they haven't shown us what they look like. The only ones we've seen, so far, look like normal women.'

'Oh, yeah,' mocked Tom. 'If they are aliens does this look like any planet you've seen pictures of?' he said, irritation and impatience clear in his voice.

Alex looked out of the window. He had to admit that the view outside wasn't like anything in his science fiction magazines, or when they'd put men on the moon. The landscape looked absolutely, boringly and predictably 'normal'.

'Have you asked them why we are here?' Alex asked changing the subject, he didn't want them arguing between themselves.

'What do you think?' Tom said sarcastically. 'We are not stupid. When we ask anything, they just give us funny looks, and they don't speak. They are just weird, weird, weird.'

'Yeah,' added Ben, 'the brown figures only ever work outside. They never come in here. Some women in white coats come and give us food which is absolutely revolting.' He

26

opened his mouth, stuck out his tongue and make a baulking noise. 'It looks like scrambled eggs but its green and tastes yuck.'

'Don't forget the tablets they try to give us,' reminded Tom.

'Yeah, we spit them out when they've gone 'cos they're probably poison or drugs or something,' said Ben, matter-of-factly. He lifted the corner of his mattress to show a small pile of bright red, slightly sticky pills.

It was then that Alex noticed a large glass capsule in the far comer of the room. It had a seat and headphones, with buttons, levers and lights on a small control panel.

'What's that glass thing over there?' he asked.

'Dunno,' replied Tom in a flat voice. He didn't want to discuss their stupid theory about aliens again. Alex would probably think they were transportation machines like you see in *'Star Trek'*.

Alex looked about the room, trying to make sense of what had happened to them. Why had they been brought here, to wherever 'here' was, by these strange beings, aliens or not? Although he was pleased to see Tom and Ben and felt happier now, they were all together, he was eager to solve the mystery. Perhaps there was a rational explanation but he couldn't think of one right now.

Chapter 3
Captives

Alex glanced down at his watch. Half an hour had passed.

'When do you see the" white coats" ?' he asked. He was feeling interested in meeting his captors at last.

Maybe they could overpower them when they came in and make a run for it. After all, there were enough of them and they were probably strong enough.

'They'll probably come in with food later on. That's the only time we saw them yesterday. Oh! And when they came in with the tablets at bedtime,' Ben said.

'I heard them come in during the night, you were asleep, Ben, but when I raised my head to look, they went away,' said Tom.

Alex walked over to the door. Its upper half was glass – he pressed his nose up against it before trying the handle. Tom sneered.

'It's locked. I suppose you think we are daft enough not to have thought of trying that.'

Alex didn't respond but still tried to peer through the glass. He suddenly straightened. He still had the knife!

A smile spread across his face and he beamed at Tom and Ben.

'Do you think they will hear if I smash the glass?' he said, proudly holding up the knife which he'd slid from his pocket.

'They might. Don't know how far away anyone is. The brown ones are outside so they won't hear,' Tom said looking slightly anxious.

'Well, we'll have to chance it. We're not staying here,' Alex said feeling quite determined to be out of the room to find out exactly where they were. He'd given up any ideas about aliens, though. Alex knew Tom was right but wasn't about to admit that this didn't seem like an alien planet.

Alex kept the knife in its sheath and held it at the blade end. He hit the glass sharply with the butt of the knife, it cracked and with another hard knock, he managed to shatter it completely. He wasted no time in clearing most of the glass out of the frame using the tip of the sheath.

'Here, put some sheets over it. We don't want to bleed to death getting out,' suggested Ben, who by now was trembling at the thought of what faced them in their escape.

Tom was already dragging a chair towards the door. 'Shh…Wait!' whispered Alex. He grabbed the folded sheet that Ben was proffering and laid it over the frame. Then he put his arm over and felt around on the other side of the door.

'Yay! The key is still in the lock. C'mon, let's go!' Alex flung the door open, and then looked at his friends. Why weren't they moving? Tom still looked worried, his eyes staring fixedly at the broken glass on the floor. Ben, who was standing next to Tom, gently shook him, as if trying to reassure him that everything would be okay. Alex was jumping up and down with impatience. They had to escape! They couldn't just sit here doing nothing. His adrenalin was flowing at the thought of solving this mystery. Moments later they were in the corridor, listening hard for any sound.

'I can't hear anything,' said Alex. 'Doesn't seem to be anybody up here.'

'No, not yet, but they may come soon,' Tom whispered. 'We'll have to be quick!'

Alex didn't quite know whether he wanted them to appear or not, but it would be brilliant to show those white-coated women that they couldn't just kidnap kids and get away with it. He was shaking at the thought of a battle and he had to remind himself to keep breathing.

Tom was gasping slightly too, and his head was swivelling in all directions as he looked for any sign of activity.

As they crept along the passageway, they passed several more bedrooms and a couple of bathrooms. It looked like any normal house, only much bigger than any he'd ever been in.

This was unreal! He felt his heart thumping and his pulse racing as he desperately looked for a way to escape. He'd stopped dreaming of a dramatic conquering once he realised that there were probably more of them than they could cope with. With a shudder, he recalled the 'thing' that had carried him into the machine. He/she or 'it' had seemed amazingly strong. Tom and Ben were silent, Alex could sense that they felt as edgy and anxious as he did.

None of the bedrooms were locked. They took turns to check out each one but the only windows that would open were too small for them to climb through.

At the end of the corridor, they found the stairs. Ben and Tom stood motionless, listening for any sound. Alex was still busy with one of the last bedroom doors. He tried the handle

– it was locked, but he could see two girls, about their age, fast asleep. He motioned his friends over.

He was just about to bang on the door to try and wake them when Tom grabbed his arm and squeezed it hard.

'Quick!' he breathed. 'Someone is coming up the stairs!'

'We should try and help those two,' urged Alex, 'they've probably been kidnapped as well!'

'They might just live here, but even if you're right we can't help those girls if the women catch us,' he said looking frantic.

Tom was right. Of course, he was. Alex wasn't thinking. He felt as if he'd been punched in the stomach, half of him feeling sick and the other half excited. Swiftly, they flung themselves through the door of the bedroom opposite, intending to hide under a bed, but luck was on their side. At the far end of the room was a door leading to a fire escape, and it was unlocked. *Hooray for health and safety!* Thought Alex, as he quickly opened the door. He gasped as the chill air hit his face but didn't hesitate in his hurry to get out. Tom and Ben were right behind him as they rushed down the metal stairs. Fields surrounded the house, but on the side nearest to them, only a matter of metres away was a forest. They couldn't believe their luck.

Better still, the 'brown' workers were out of sight – he hoped – on the other side of the building. Unless anyone inside the house had spotted them coming down the fire escape then no one would realise they'd gone – until they saw the empty bedroom.

At the foot of the fire escape, Alex turned briefly to look at the house. He could see now that it was a tall, imposing building the size of a large mansion.

'The trees! Come on…' He beckoned to his friends and they set off running as fast as they could across the grass. A loud siren had begun to wail and as they neared the forest, they could see the brown workers and women in white coats starting to run after them.

The 'browns' appeared to lumber along, but the women were much faster. Tom pitched forward and almost fell, but Alex and Ben both grabbed a shoulder each and hauled him upright. They had reached the trees before any of the women had come halfway across the field.

They ran on through the gloominess of the forest, tripping and stumbling over roots and fallen logs.

'C'mon! They can't catch us!' yelled Alex, though he was trying to convince himself as much as his friends that he was right.

They could still hear the women shouting in the distance.

'They can't escape from our world!' one of them yelled menacingly. 'We'll find them sooner or later.'

What does she mean, they can't escape from our world? Alex wondered. Surely this is still earth. He was panting hard with exertion but was mystified by what the woman had said. So, what 'world' were they supposed to be in?

'I wish this was a dream much as I like mysteries,' he whispered.

Tom looked over at him.

'So do I,' he responded, his voice shaking. It seemed as though they had been running forever.

They'd come through the trees and into a meadow which in turn led to another. They couldn't see anyone behind them and Alex hoped that the women had given up chasing them. Ben broke his thoughts.

'What do we do now, then?' he said in a slightly heated tone.

'I don't know, haven't got a clue,' Alex retorted. 'We need to find out where we are, who they are and who lives around here.'

He was still getting his breath back, but he knew they couldn't stay there for long. He looked around and had to admit that it certainly didn't look like another planet. The landscape and the vegetation were just the same, and the air seemed okay if a lot colder. Perhaps they weren't that far away from home after all.

Alex still would have liked to find out who these people were and why they had been taken to that big house. Maybe they would find out more when they found some people who could tell them.

'Got any bright ideas?' he asked.

Tom and Ben stared at him and shook their heads, looking to him for answers. Obviously, they had to keep going until they found help. They continued jogging, looking over their shoulders every few seconds.

Suddenly, Alex stopped.

'Wait! I can hear the sea!' he yelled. Sure enough, they could hear waves crashing not far ahead of them.

'I can see *them!*' whispered Ben.

As they turned, they saw three of the white-coats emerging from the trees and coming across the first meadow.

'Run!' shouted Alex. Tom had frozen in fear, so Alex grabbed his hand and pulled him along. They ran as fast as they could towards the sea, their legs hardly seeming to touch the ground. Slowing near the cliff top, Alex peered down and spotted a small bay down to one side.

'What now?' asked Tom, shaking all over, probably as much with the cold as with fear.

Alex glanced at them both, he was trying desperately to think and catch his breath at the same time. There must be somewhere…

'Look!' Alex pointed. 'A footpath, it must go down to the beach.'

They set off at a run, feet slipping slightly on the screen. As they rounded a corner Alex glanced up and stopped short. There across the bay was a lighthouse. It looked familiar somehow. He put it to the back of his mind and carried on running. Once they were down on the sand, they could find a cave or a rock crevice to hide in. They had to hope that these women wouldn't reach the edge of the cliff before that, otherwise, they would be seen, and then who knew?

Once on the beach, the boys kept close to the rocks, looking for somewhere to hide.

'Here, quick. Get inside!' Alex whispered. There was a small cave in the rock, just big enough for them to squeeze inside whilst they got their breath back and think about what they were to do next. Puffing and panting, Alex peered out from their hiding place.

Suddenly, he spotted a dark shape nestled nearby amongst the rocks.

'Look! A little rowing boat! If we're quick we can reach it before they get down here,' he gasped.

Moments later, they were dragging the boat across the sand. They pushed it into the sea and jumped in. Alex and Ben took the oars and rowed as fast as they could. Tom was motionless, staring back at the women, who by now had reached the water's edge. He watched as they started to wade out towards them. Alex saw them too; he was hoping that they weren't very good swimmers.

As they rowed out to sea, along the coast, Alex exhaled, when he realised that the white coats couldn't reach them. He prodded Tom to bring him out of his trance-like state. The women had stopped and were shaking their fists. He could just hear them shouting at them that they wouldn't get away, before turning around and going back up the beach.

Alex was deep in thought, trying to ignore the ache in his shoulders from rowing so hard.

'What's the matter?' asked Tom who had started to look less anxious. He looked up.

'I thought that lighthouse looked familiar,' he told them, 'I know where we are, now! It's St Bees Lighthouse. That was Fleswick Bay down from St Bees Head. I've been here with mum and dad loads of times.' He grinned and punched the air with his clenched fist. Ben was frowning.

'So?' he said. 'How does that help us exactly?'

'Don't you see? If we carry on round the comer to St Bees, we're not that far from home,' he said triumphantly.

Now it was Tom's turn to frown.

'I don't get it, though. If we're so near home, why did they bring us here in that weird machine? They could have just used a car.'

'You're asking questions I don't know the answers to. Yes, it seems strange but we are definitely not far from…'

Alex's voice drifted away. He was thinking about what the woman had said 'they can't escape from our world!'

Chapter 4
Father Williams

The current was with them now, and the boat bobbed easily down the coast towards St Bees Head. Not far from there was the village of St Bees, and, they hoped, safety. They were incredibly tired. All of them had rowed boats before many times. They were used to rowing a little boat on Keswick Lake, but they'd never rowed for this long and never at sea.

The relief they felt when they pulled the boat on to the beach was enormous. They set off at a brisk pace towards the village. As they walked, all three of them started to shiver. Not with fear, this time, but with cold. Apart from the initial chill of the wind as they escaped from the building, they hadn't noticed the difference in temperature. Now, though, their teeth were chattering. Their tee shirts were useless against the cold.

The village wasn't how Alex remembered it at all. There were a lot more houses and little shops where before there had only been fields or car parks.

Two young women were walking towards them, suitably dressed in coats, hats and scarves against the chill. Although they stared at the three boys neither of them spokes to them.

'Probably on holiday from somewhere,' Alex heard one say to the other. The other one nodded and commented on their lack of dress for the weather.

As they walked on, they spotted the primary school.

It was different, somehow. It looked as though it had been extended at some time, but now it seemed dilapidated and empty. He recognised the statue of Saint Bees – he knew from school that she was the Irish nun from which the village took its name.

As they passed the houses Alex thought about knocking on someone's door but realised that this may not be such a good idea. His parents had warned him often enough not to approach anyone he didn't know. He could hear his dad now.

'There are too many bad people in the world today, son. If you are ever lost or stuck somewhere and need help, find a police station.'

His dad! Alex hadn't thought until now. How would his father have felt when he watched him being taken without being able to help? Oh, and his mum – she would be yelling and wailing blaming his poor dad for agreeing to stay out in the pasture and she wouldn't understand what he had seen…their son being taken by something and then disappearing. His poor dad…

As they walked through the village, Alex tried to spot a police station. They saw some more women who also stared at them as they passed, whispering to each other. On reflection, Alex thought it a bit strange they hadn't seen any men or children. Okay, the school must be out, but surely there would be kids playing outside.

'The nearest one will be in Whitehaven,' Alex said suddenly.

'The nearest what?' asked Tom. 'What about Whitehaven?'

'Sorry. Thinking out aloud,' grinned Alex. 'We ought to find a police station but the nearest one will probably be in Whitehaven.'

'What about a church, then?' Ben suggested.

'Yeah,' said Alex, 'something's not quite right…'

He felt very uneasy but knew they needed to tell someone about what had happened, and perhaps get some answers too.

'You probably can't get much safer than a vicar,' agreed Tom. He looked much calmer than he had been since they'd run from the house. He thought for a moment or two.

'Wonder if the vicar's a woman? We haven't seen a man since we got here.'

'Haven't seen any kids either except for those two girls at the house,' Ben remarked.

The church was empty but there were candles lit around the alter. They trod carefully down to the front and sat in one of the pews. They suddenly felt very weary. Hours seemed to have passed since their escape from the big house.

Alex glanced at the clock on the wall at the back. Still over an hour until noon. He was tired, cold and hungry. Yawning, he looked at his friends who seemed ready to fall asleep right where they were.

'I'm too tired to do anything else,' he said. 'We'll be safe in here for a bit, won't we?' he nodded at the others. They talked for a while, trying to make sense of what had happened until Alex got up to stretch his legs, and try and find something warm to put on – he was freezing. As he wandered around, he spotted a newspaper on a chair just inside the vestry. Both Tom and Ben heard his gasp and came running.

'This can't be right!' he exclaimed. He had the paper in one hand and was trying, unsuccessfully, to clean his glasses with the other.

'What?' Tom asked as Ben looked over Alex's shoulder.

'This paper, the date is wrong! It says it's the end of November 2070!' He held it under their noses.

Sure enough, the date was as clear as day 26th November 2070.

'Of course, it's wrong,' said Ben. 'It's got to be!'

'No son, I'm afraid it isn't.' Said a deep voice behind them. 'It is without a doubt the 26th day of November 2070. Just under a month until Christmas.'

They gawped at him. It was definitely the vicar and he was definitely a man. He had a neat, white beard and a big booming voice. Alex stood with his mouth open.

'What's the matter?' he asked. 'Don't tell me you've forgotten what date it is.'

The boys continued to stare at him, confusion on their faces and lost for words.

'Come on, what's up, boys?' he repeated.

'Well…the date…it can't be right, it's only 2010,' Alex protested, his voice high and choked. The vicar sighed, then gently led the boys back to the pews. He sat them down and confirmed that they were truly in the year 2070. Alex went pale. The words of the white-coat came back to him… 'They can't escape from our world.'

The vicar interrupted his thoughts.

'I don't understand this,' he said. 'Are you playing some kind of joke? I know you are not from around here, but where are your parents, hmm? And why on earth are you all in tee shirts? It's not very warm out there today.'

Alex blinked a couple of times before launching into their story, starting with his first sighting of one of the 'browns' in their pasture. The vicar sat silently and listened throughout. He remained silent for a moment or two, rubbing his chin. His eyes narrowed as he looked suspiciously at the boys in front of him.

'Unbelievable!' he murmured. 'So, you are telling me that you were all taken in a machine to a big house near St Bees and you're all from farms near Keswick? That house you are describing sounds like the Institute, the Scientific Institute for Research. Hmmm...'

'Well, what kind of research do they do?' Alex asked-he couldn't take this in. Had they been brought to this place by time travel? Surely that was all science fiction – but maybe it wouldn't be in the future...this future?

'Oh, they do all kinds of research. They were the first to find a cure for Alzheimer's disease, but I don't know what they are working on now, though, genetics, I think?'

Alex knew what Alzheimer's was – his uncle had started to lose his memory a couple of years ago and nobody had been able to help him. It was getting worse and now he couldn't even remember his own friends and relatives. He had heard his mum talk about his uncle having 'walkabout episodes' outside, in the middle of the night in his pyjamas, and that he would have to go into a care home so that he could be looked after properly.

'Oh, I forgot!' exclaimed the vicar. 'I'm sorry, I'm Father Williams, pleased to meet you, boys.' He offered his hand. The boys frowned but shook his hand and gave him their names.

'Um…you're the only man we've seen so far and there are no kids, either. Is there something going on here?'

Father Williams sighed. 'I was about to ask you three the same question. Are you telling me some sort of tale? Surely you must know what has been happening here?'

The looks on their faces told him that they weren't joking he sat down heavily on a nearby chair.

'Six months ago, St Bees was put into quarantine after a virus hit the community. All the children died. Because of these problems most of the families, men and women, moved to Whitehaven. Only a handful of females have remained behind, single women, old and young. You three are the only youngsters I've seen in the village for some time.'

No wonder those women they saw were staring at them, Alex thought. He understood why now.

'Did this happen everywhere, Father Williams?' Alex asked.

'No, only here. The virus was found in locally- grown food, from the Institute. Fruit and vegetables had become so expensive they started to grow their own on the allotments. They traced the problem to some fertiliser they were using at the time…but I'm sure you will have already heard about that, surely?' He gave them a stern look.

'No! We don't even belong here so how could we have known?' said Alex. 'I've told you what happened to us. Do you think we are lying?' He looked at the vicar straight in the eyes. Father Williams didn't reply- he stood up and started to tum away.

Alex, however, was determined to get some answers. 'So, if there aren't any men here, why have you stayed? Must be strange living in a place where there aren't any other blokes.' He shuddered at the thought of a world full of only women.

'I have a job to do, son. I can't just leave my parish. The women still come to church on Sundays. Even if I don't like what has happened.' He took a deep breath. 'Right then if you are all finished, I have some work to do. So, if you will excuse me, boys.'

He didn't know where these boys had come from but they could surely spin an incredible tale. He turned away from the boys once more. Alex was feeling really cross. Why did adults have this infuriating habit of not believing anything you said? He drew himself up to his full height.

'Father Williams, sir,' he said through gritted teeth. 'What about the two girls we told you about? You said there were no children in St Bees, so how do you explain that? And why have we been dragged away from our homes?'

Father Williams raised his eyebrows – they didn't seem bad lads but you never knew these days. He sat down again. 'Hold on, lads. You ask too many questions and I can't begin to explain what has happened to you. I can't even be sure that you're telling me the truth, it seems so far-fetched.' He scratched his head. 'The Institute is a reputable place. Never had any trouble with them. Why should anyone believe your accusations? Those girls are obviously there for good reason, they are probably relatives of one of the staff who come to visit from outside the area.'

Alex was breathing hard.

'Okay, how do you explain us being yanked 60 years into the future? We just don't belong here!' Alex was trying very hard not to shout. Tom and Ben were staring open-mouthed at him.

'I can't explain anything. Perhaps I should take you back to the Institute and get some answers from them,' he said. He hoped that this bluff would bring out the truth.

'We are not going back there. Never!' Alex said shaking his head. 'They took us away from our homes, I've told you.'

Tom, who had been silent all the while, closed his mouth and then immediately opened it again.

'What are we going to do, Father Williams?' he pleaded. 'We just want to go back home,' he said with unshed tears in his eyes.

'I'm sorry, boys. I don't know what I can do to help. I suppose the police should be the first port of call. You can stay at the rectory in the meantime, there's plenty of room. Come on.' Father Williams strode away and the three boys walked obediently behind him. The vicar still didn't know what to make of their story, and in a way, he was playing along with them. Sooner or later, they would admit it was a joke, surely?

Alex knew full well that Father Williams didn't believe a word he'd said, but they followed him to the rectory. What else could they do? He hoped the police would be a bit more helpful. The vicar seemed a nice man and he supposed that their story did sound incredible.

The rectory turned out to be an old, but well-maintained bungalow. Once through the porch, there was a dimly lit passage, off which were several different rooms. The kitchen was at the far end.

'Are you hungry?' he said as they reached the large kitchen.

'Yes, starving, we haven't eaten since yesterday,' Alex replied.

Father Williams took no time at all in preparing a meal of sausage and orange-coloured mashed potato. They made short work of it – it felt as though they hadn't eaten for weeks. They hadn't realised how hungry they were.

Chapter 5
Sergeant Tripp

After they had eaten, Father Williams called the police station. An officer, Sergeant Tripp, called to interview them about an hour later. He was a big man, and obviously not used to spending any time on the beat. He sat gently wheezing as they told him their story. He was clearly finding it very hard to keep a straight face and burst out laughing once they had finished their tale.

'What are you laughing at?' Alex clenched his fists.

He could feel his pulse racing and his face reddening. 'You asked us what happened, hasn't anyone told you that it's rude to laugh at people when they are being serious?' He didn't care anymore what his parents had drummed into him about being polite to adults. He could not fathom why no one would believe them – just because they were kids!

'Why am I laughing, sonny? It's because I've never heard such rubbish in all my life. The Institute does some really important research. They wouldn't get involved in anything like you are telling me. These are very serious allegations you are making, laddie.'

Alex was too angry for words. He scowled at the sergeant, then turned to his friends. They just looked at him, eyes wide, and mouths agape.

'Right, lads, I want to know where your parents are so that I can—'

Alex cut him short, shaking with anger and frustration.

'Yes. And WE want to know where our parents are, too! DON'T YOU UNDERSTAND? I told you our parents are in another time zone, 60 years ago. What can't you understand?'

'We'll have less of that, lad. Obviously, your parents haven't taught you to be respectful to your elders.'

Alex knew the officer was right, his mum and dad would be really angry with him for being rude.

'I'm sorry…but honestly we're not making this up,' he said more quietly. His chest was aching with tension but he knew that if he continued venting his anger he would probably get nowhere. He knew only too well that you couldn't win with adults.

'We'll get to the bottom of this. I'll visit the Institute right now and check it out,' he said with a sigh. Alex caught him winking at Father Williams.

'We're coming with you,' Alex said, he guessed Sergeant Tripp wouldn't discover anything otherwise.

'No! You can stay right here with the father until I get back, thank you very much.' He looked at Father Williams, who nodded in agreement. 'I don't want any of you causing any trouble and making wild accusations.'

Alex shrugged. There was no point in arguing. He reckoned the police would probably have a good laugh about it all. The sergeant was only going to the Institute because he was duty-bound to investigate any allegations. Anything to do with children was to be taken seriously, apparently, that's why he, a sergeant, had been assigned to them, and not some lowly constable. That didn't mean Tripp would put much effort into it. He wondered how much trouble they'd be in for wasting police time. Time…yeah, now that was a joke.

While they waited for the officer to return none of them had much to say. Alex had dreamed about solving a real-life mystery but not like this one. He was becoming truly fed up with it all and just wished they could go home.

It was over an hour later when the sergeant returned.

He didn't look pleased and he glared at them all. 'Just as I thought, a total waste of time. I spoke with Miss Blackwood at the Institute and had a good look around. In fact, she was only too pleased to show me. There was definitely no machine like you described anywhere, either in the house or their laboratory.'

'Yes, that's because they can make it invisible. What's the point anyway, you don't believe us,' Alex retorted, a flicker of irritation in his voice.

'Look, I've heard enough of this. It's bad enough I've got to find somewhere for you to stay until we find your parents.'

'Good luck with that,' Alex muttered, then spoke up. 'So, what about the other children in the house?' He already knew there would be a plausible explanation.

'As I said, we searched the premises. We found no children at all in the Institute. Miss Blackwood was more than helpful.'

'She probably made them invisible as well,' Alex said. Ben and Tom sniggered their hands over their mouths. He knew that Sergeant Tripp probably wouldn't have looked around properly, as he didn't believe their story anyway, but kept his thoughts quiet.

'Right. That's it I've heard enough. Gracious knows how long it will take to sort out somewhere for you all to stay. Thanks to you three I have enough paperwork to last the rest of the evening.'

Father Williams, who had been listening to all that had been said with interest, smiled at the sergeant.

'They can stay here overnight if it helps. It is getting late after all.'

The officer sighed. 'I suppose that would be better, it is nearly five. Thank you, Father Williams, you have been more than helpful. I'll pick them up first thing in the morning. I'll get their photographs taken and after I've checked missing person reports, I'll put them out in the press and the internet.'

With that, he put his cap back on his head, turned on his heel and walked out.

Alex couldn't believe the sergeant's attitude. He didn't care what he thought, they weren't making anything up and he was determined, if possible, to discover the facts with or without anyone's help, except his friends.

That night they were all very subdued. They'd eaten a meal of sandwiches and crisps, washed down with a glass of milk, and then sat in the warmth of the living room. Father Williams had found them some winter clothes from a pile of donations he had been given after all the children had died. Oh, what a time that had been. He'd kept the clothes, goodness knows why when there were no children to hand those over to at the present time, but you never knew when they would come in useful in the future. People would start having babies again.

As they sat there, Alex wondered what his parents must be going through. He could only imagine how upset they would be. He tried to go over all the events logically, but none of it made any sense. It was with a heavy heart that he realised they may never get back home again. He'd often imagined being on an adventure away from home and solving some mystery or other, but now he longed to be in his own bed. He felt defeated for the first time in his life.

He hadn't realised how tired he was until they trooped along the passageway to what would be their beds for the night. The three of them were asleep almost as soon as their heads touched the pillows. Alex dreamed of floating in the air, his dad trying desperately to reach him. Every time their hands came within touching distance, Alex had been raised further up into the sky. Then he couldn't see his father anymore. Alex woke the next morning feeling exhausted. He had a dull feeling in his chest, which ached, and his throat was sore as if he had been crying all night. Tom and Ben looked how he felt.

They were still finishing their breakfast when Sergeant Tripp arrived. Good as his word, he'd come to take them to the police station in Whitehaven. The boys all thanked Father Williams for letting them stay, taking turns to shake his hand.

'I do hope you find your parents,' was all he said as they walked away down the path, shoulders hunched and trailing their feet. Alex turned and gave him a half smile; he wished the father had believed them. A few minutes later, they were in the back of the police car staring out of the window. Alex turned to his friends and whispered.

'How's he ever going to find our parents? They'll be turned 90 by now and maybe even dead,' he whispered, shuddering at this awful thought.

'That means we'll never see them again if we can't go back,' Tom said, blinking hard to stop the tears from coming.

'What are you whispering about?' snapped sergeant Tripp.

'We were just saying we doubt you'll find our parents as they will be in their nineties by now and probably dead.' Ben told him. He could see that this realisation had hit them all and Tom and Alex were doing their best not to cry.

'Look! I've honestly had enough of this stupid childish behaviour. You might as well tell me the truth right now and save us all a lot of time,' he demanded.

'We are telling you the truth, we are not lying,' Alex yelled, his voice cracking.

The boys looked at each other in despair. Sergeant Tripp pressed a button on the dashboard and a glass partition slid up from behind the front seats. He pressed another button and the glass become opaque. He'd clearly had enough of them.

At the police station, they were put in a room opposite the custody desk. An officer came in, took a couple of photographs of them and told them to wait quietly until the sergeant returned.

'What are we going to do now?' Ben asked tearfully.

'I dunno, do I?' shrugged Alex. 'They're not going to find our parents so we might as well try and escape and do it all ourselves.' He was feeling slightly braver now.

'Yeah, and how do we get out of here?' Tom asked.

He was thinking that Alex must be off his head for even suggesting this. *How were they going to get past the policeman behind the custody desk? Had he completely lost his marbles?* Alex ignored him and opened the door a fraction. He could see the officer behind the counter, and beyond that, two other officers sitting at desks with their backs to them, working on computers. Alex put his fingers to his lips.

'When I say move, move,' he whispered. They stared at him, speechless, surely, they would be caught as soon as they stepped out of the room.

Alex waited until the officer behind the front desk stood up and walked behind one of his colleagues who had alerted him to something on the computer. He crouched down, beckoning Tom and Ben, he motioned them to get in front of him, he would follow up the rear hoping that the door didn't make a noise when it closed. They crawled on all fours towards the front door keeping close to the front desk. The front door opened with a loud creak, and the officer spun around.

'Hey, come back!' he shouted, as the boys stood up and bolted into the street.

Chapter 6
The Institute

They ran as fast as their legs would carry them. Alex thought briefly about going into one of the shops to hide but guessed they would probably be handed straight over to the police. He could hear heavy footsteps closing in behind them and hardly dared to look back over his shoulder. One of the policemen had caught up with Ben and grabbed his jacket collar – the jacket Father Williams had given him. Both Alex and Tom held their breath and froze momentarily as Ben struggled to rid himself of the jacket. Two other officers were still running a little way behind, they were nowhere near as fit as the boys. After a brief tussle, when Ben managed to leave his jacket behind in the hands of the police officer, they took off down side street after side street – weaving in and out until they could no longer hear anyone behind them. All the same, they didn't stop running until they reached the harbour. Tom bent forward, his hands on his knees…trying to get his breath back. Alex and Ben leaned against a wall, panting.

"What do we do now?" Tom gasped. He looked at Alex as if running away was the dumbest idea ever.

"We are going back to the Institute to prove there's something going on there," he replied.

"Have you gone stark raving mad, Alex?" Ben yelled; he didn't like this idea one bit." Why don't we just go back to Keswick?"

"No point, is there? We have already discussed this. They are probably already dead by now." he said again, shuddering at the thought.

"How far is that place?" asked Tom. They were all tired from the run. Fortunately, though, they all loved any kind of sport, no matter what it was and had lots of stamina.

"Not that far. There's a footpath over the cliffs from here to the beach at St Bees onto Fleswick Bay. After that, we just have to go up the cliff again and across to the Institute. We can probably make it there in a few hours if we get a move on," he said making it sound like the easiest thing in the world. Tom was thinking, he didn't know what they could prove once they reached the Institute. Probably, no one was going to believe them even if they did find anything.

Alex was thinking that if they managed to find the machine they had travelled in, they could get back home…it was a thought he had to hang onto to keep their spirits up.

"C'mon, it's mid-morning already, we need to get going."

As they walked along the coastal path, Alex allowed himself to smile. They had given the police the slip and now they might actually make some progress.

"The police probably think we've gone to find our parents in Keswick. They'll never in a million years think we've come back to the Institute," he remarked smugly.

By noon they were hungry and thirsty. Alex wished they could have got some provisions from one of the shops they had passed earlier but this would have been too risky.

They all felt about ready to collapse from exhaustion but no one said anything – none of them wanted to appear like a wimp. They finally arrived at St Bees Head and struggled across to Fleswick Bay, their legs aching. The climb back up, the cliff was tough going and they were all really tired making their way back to the forest. The rough grass lay in large clumps which made walking difficult. At the edge of the trees, they were pleased to find some blackberries, albeit a bit soggy, as well as some beech nuts and the odd hazelnut, or filbert, as Alex liked to call them. None of it was exactly filling, but it staved off the boys' hunger pangs, a little. They plodded wearily to the edge of the forest and peered out of the undergrowth at the Institute. Alex was pleased to see that there was no one in sight. The 'browns' would be on the other side of the house.

"I know we are all tired but if we can manage to run towards the house, without anyone seeing us, we can get back in using the fire escape," he said crossing his fingers. He was keen to get to the bottom of all this, and getting caught was the last thing they needed.

They reached the house, without incident – the side of the building they were on had all the blinds closed, except for one – the lights were on and the blinds partly drawn. Hardly daring to breathe, Alex snook up to the window and stared in. He could see a small group of 'white-coats' sitting at a large table…they were eating. It was then that he saw the two girls.

"Look!" he whispered." It's those two girls we saw…"

Nervously, Tom and Ben straightened up and peered through the window.

"Hmm…not sure," replied Ben," but if it is them, they don't seem very bothered." He could see that the girls were interacting with the women, laughing and talking with each other as if they belonged there.

"Perhaps I was wrong and they haven't been abducted."

"Yeah, but remember they don't have any children at all so where have they come from?" asked Tom.

"Unless they are relatives coming to visit but the sergeant said he hadn't seen any children," he replied.

They stood and watched for a while before Alex whispered." If they're all in there eating, now it's a good time to go up the fire escape and look for any proof in the house. We might find that machine they transported us in"

"I dunno, Alex. What if they catch us again?" Tom said looking around. He didn't relish the thought of being in the company of that sergeant again, much less in the hands of the 'white-coats'. Apart from anything else, that long walk back here would have been for nothing.

"Don't you want to find out what has been happening?" Alex said in a low voice." We need some kind of evidence for the police. Then they might be able to get us back home. You do want to get back home, don't you?"

Ben nodded in agreement, but Tom was still not convinced. He knew there was probably no other way for them to get home, but he could just imagine them being in a lot of trouble to boot.

So it was with some reluctance that he followed Alex and Ben as they sidled up the fire escape. The top door was still unlocked, and there didn't seem to be anyone around. The first place they checked where they had seen the girls was empty as were all the remaining rooms on that floor. Alex frowned. Had those two girls been the ones they'd seen sleeping, or not?

Tom Interrupted his thoughts." We've seen the girls but there's no way of telling anyone that they are here and we don't even know whether they were abducted like us. Doesn't look like it, and, I definitely don't fancy walking all the way back to Whitehaven."

Alex nodded." Neither do I. Perhaps there is a phone around here somewhere."

They crept around the upstairs bedrooms but found nothing except a glass contraption they had seen in their bedroom. The 'browns' were still outside working. They went down to the lower floor, wincing at every little sound they made. The first room they came to was absolutely huge. It had one wall completely lined with books, and there were desks with computers and printers but no phones. The room opposite was just as large and contained sofas, chairs and the most enormous television screen on the wall they had ever seen. They plonked down on one of the sofas, suddenly realising how really tired they were. Alex closed his eyes, desperately trying to think what they could do next. It all seemed so hopeless. There didn't appear to be any way they could contact the police and he didn't really want to have to go all the way back to St Bees, as the sergeant from Whitehaven would probably lock them up. How was he going to prove that there were girls here. Ben startled him out of his reverie…

"Perhaps they only use mobiles now," he suggested.

There was only one more room to investigate on the floor. Feeling quite disheartened, Alex led the way through the door. They all stopped dead in their tracks at what they saw. The room was long and narrow, with metalwork benches along one side. Upon these were test tubes, monitors and various other scientific equipment, but what caught their attention were the six very large glass contraptions along the opposite wall.

"I wonder what they use those for?" Ben said, going over to have a look. He opened the door of the nearest one but was startled by Alex pulling him away.

"What are you doing?" Alex asked." Crikey, don't go inside. We don't know what they do. Probably brain-scramblers for all we know."

Something else, however had caught Alex's eye. The whole of the bottom wall was covered with a thick dark curtain. He wandered over and pulled the curtain to one side. This wasn't a wall covering, it was a partition. The huge space behind the curtain was completely empty! He stepped forward but was stopped by some kind of barrier he couldn't see but could feel. He turned around to his friends – shock on his face.

"It's solid, some kind of invisible shield, look feel!" he said as Ben and Tom stepped forward to investigate. Tom rubbed his head.

"What's the point of having an invisible shield for an empty space behind it? It doesn't make any sense..." He rubbed his head again.

"Yes! Of course, the machine is in there and it's invisible, can't be any other explanation," said Alex. His heart beat with excitement at the idea. That's why they hadn't seen it when they were abducted and the sergeant hadn't seen it either. He just hoped he was right...very clever, he thought, if it was true.

"I think we'd better scarper," said Ben," we don't know whether we are being watched, or even if there is some kind of detection alarm in here."

They left the room, and for want of anywhere else to go, went into the room with the sofas – they were all so tired. Alex was almost overwhelmed with the desire to sleep. His eyes had just begun to droop when they heard the sound of light footsteps. They sprung to their feet as the two girls – of a similar age to them – stepped into the room. They stared at each other for what seemed an age until Alex spoke.

"Who are you?" he asked trying to sound calm.

"Uh, no, who are you?" It was the taller of the two girls, she was scowling but looked rather pretty, with long dark hair and piercing blue eyes.

Alex had to think quickly, he didn't want to raise any suspicions but he also wanted some answers from them.

"Oh, we're just visiting my aunt," he said, blushing slightly.

"Oh!" she said turning to the other girl.

"Can't remember you two, though the last time we visited," Alex continued, crossing his fingers behind his back.

The other girl, who had short blonde curly hair, looked puzzled. Yea.

"Have you been here long?" Alex asked.

"What do you mean? We have always lived here with our mothers," she replied, a look of confusion on her face.

Alex tried not to show surprise. Father Williams had said all the children had died. Tom and Ben were quietly watching the dialogue between Alex and the taller girl. There appeared to be an unspoken agreement that Alex would do the talking. However, Alex had stopped talking, his mind racing with questions but he also knew that they had to get away before anyone else discovered them.

Ben and Tom were staring at Alex, willing him to say or do something, anything before these girls – dippy as they looked – realised something was up.

"Well," said Alex, with a forced smile," it's been nice meeting you both but we have to return home, to Whitehaven now. Perhaps we'll see each other again."

Ben and Tom heaved a sigh of relief, but continued to look intently at Alex, willing him to make a move and quickly.

The girls stared at them as Alex led the way to the door…too late! One if the 'white-coats' was approaching fast. Alex stepped abruptly backwards, nearly bowling his friends over.

 The 'white-coat' strode into the room and then stopped short. She stared briefly at the boys before turning her attention to the girls.

"Adrianne, Felicity, you are needed downstairs to help with the clearing away."

"Mother, these boys—"

"Can you do that please?" she said, in a tone that brooked no argument.

Alex knew that kind of tone only too well. His parents used it regularly – he held his breath. The woman waited until the girls had left before she spoke again. It was clear she was very angry.

"So, you've decided to come back after all the trouble you've caused!" she said in a quiet but menacing voice. Her eyes darted impatiently from one boy to another.

Alex started to speak but she raised her hand to silence him. She put her head to one side.

"In here!" she shouted. Another 'white-coat' entered the room and looked them up and down.

"What are we going to do with them?"

"Well, we can't keep them here, the police know about them now," she replied calmly." We'll ring Sergeant Tripp, we fooled him before, we can do it again quite easily," she said in a low voice.

She brought a very small black device from her pocket, tapped a few times and spoke into it.

"Sergeant Tripp, please, it's Miss Blackwood."

Whilst she was busy talking, Alex turned his attention to the other woman who was still glaring at them.

"So, she's Adrianne's mother then!" Alex said mockingly, suddenly feeling brave. He raised his eyebrows in disbelief. Ben kicked his shin and he jumped.

Miss Blackwood ended her call at that point and Alex didn't get any reply to his statement.

"He's coming over to get them," she said.

Determined to get an answer, Alex looked her in the eyes.

"Where did those girls come from?" he asked feeling that he had nothing to lose." We were told there were no children in St Bees."

"None of your business," she snapped, poking him in the chest with her sharp fingernail.

Undeterred, Alex continued," We know there aren't any children in St Bees and the girls told us they lived here with their mothers," he said pointedly.

She narrowed her eyes at him and didn't speak for a few seconds.

"Don't assume the police are going to believe any more of your stupid little stories." Miss Blackwood snapped. They left the room, locking the door behind them. That's right, just like an adult, change the subject, thought Alex

Alex went to the door and pressed his ear against it. He could hear Miss Blackwood talking to the other woman.

"Better make sure the girls are nowhere to be seen when the police arrive. Get Martha to take them down to the cellar again. Sergeant Tripp won't try too hard to find them. I get the impression he's pretty fed up with those boys. He's not going to believe anything they say."

Alex could hear them laughing as they went downstairs to the ground floor.

"Something really weird is going on in here," he said turning to his friends.

"I knew we shouldn't have come back," Tom said, looking crossly at Alex.

"Sergeant Tripp has to believe us now," he said, but secretly he wasn't very hopeful.

"That story of us visiting your aunt was a scream, though quick thinking," said Ben laughing. At least he was seeing the funny side of the situation.

Tom didn't look at all amused. He walked over to the window and gazed out at the dull landscape. About half an hour later, Sergeant Tripp entered the room with the two women who remained close to the door. Sergeant Tripp approached the boys, his face red and the veins in his neck positively bulging.

" I don't know what you're playing at boys," he boomed," but I am getting very, VERY tired of this whole business."

Alex opened his mouth to speak but was cut short as the sergeant stepped in front of him, putting his face so close to his that their noses were practically touching.

"I don't want any more of your stories, my lad," he said through clenched teeth. Spittle flew from his mouth, hitting Alex in the face.

"But—" he said and had to step back to avoid Sergeant Tripp knocking him over.

"I said NO MORE!"

Alex was not about to give up, he was determined to speak and bawled loudly at the Sergeant.

"There are two girls here! We've been talking to them and I overheard Miss Blackwood saying—"

"That's enough!" he said grabbing hold of Alex roughly by his collar.

Tom turned from the window and marched over to the pair of them. He stood firmly in front of the, officer glaring at him intently.

"They are here, we all saw them. They're hiding them out of the way so you don't find them, you stupid man," he bellowed…and asked them what's in that other room, behind the curtain, wrenching Alex from the sergeant's grip.

Alex and Ben couldn't believe what they were hearing. This was nothing like Tom – he never lost his temper or spoke to anyone like that – especially not an adult.

Sergeant Tripp didn't respond but let out a sigh and turned back to the two women.

"Leave them with me for a moment please," he said. Alex looked at the women and noticed that they were looking quite worried, their eyes fixed and staring but quickly planted a false smile on their faces when the Sergeant nodded to them to leave the room.

"I went to Keswick when you ran off from the police station. As I suspected, your parents don't live at Rook Farm or anywhere else in Keswick. The young woman who lives there told me that they had been there for the past five years and didn't know you or your parents, lad," he said, looking at Alex.

"I've told you. They will probably be dead by now. This is 2070 and we live in 2010.!"

"I don't suppose you asked about Ben and me," Tom butted in, the adrenalin still whirring about in his body.

"No, I didn't. Having proved that I was on a wild goose chase, I didn't want to waste any more time on this, this ridiculous story. It's quite obvious that you are all runaways from somewhere but we'll find out the truth in the end."

Tom looked at Alex, who shook his head and shrugged.

"Until we've made further enquiries as to the whereabouts of your parents, Father Williams has kindly offered to let you stay with him. However, I'm warning you that if you try to cause any more trouble, I'll take you back to the police station. Do I make myself perfectly clear?" he demanded.

Alex refused to answer him but instead kept his head down, staring at his feet.

As Sergeant Tripp escorted them out of the house, he apologised to Miss Blackwood for any trouble they had been put to. She nodded to him, barely able to keep the smug look off her face. This infuriated Alex and he turned sharply towards the Sergeant.

"They are in the cellar!" he shouted in a last ditch attempt to get his attention.

Miss Blackwood sighed and said," We don't have a cellar in this building, but you are welcome to look about the place again," she said with a sweet sickly grin on her face.

"I'm sure that won't be necessary, Miss Blackwood. Thank you again for your help in this unfortunate matter."

"If you ask my opinion, these children must have suffered sone kind of trauma to result in this kind of behaviour," she said as the sergeant led them towards the car.

Alex said nothing. What was the use? Sergeant Tripp would never believe them in a million years. They were only kids – aftcr all.

Chapter 7
A Way Out

During the journey to the church, nobody spoke. Alex felt it would be useless to say anything more to the sergeant. He'd made his mind up without even checking what they'd told him about the girls. *It wasn't fair*, he thought but knew that no one would believe a group of children over that of a scientist. They had no chance of convincing anyone of the truth. On arrival at the rectory, Father Williams was waiting for them and he smiled somewhat sympathetically at them − he put his hand on Alex's shoulder.

'Don't let them out of your sight, Father,' the Sergeant told him. 'Find them something useful to do. Keep them out of trouble. I feel sure that we will find their parents once we put their photos in the media.'

They all remained quiet until the sergeant had left. 'Lads, what have you all been up to? You are in a lot of trouble.'

Alex told Father Williams everything that had happened at the Institute but he just looked at them in despair.

'Father Williams, we're not telling lies, honest. I wish someone would just believe what we're saying,' he said. He felt so discouraged and hopeless.

'You must realise that what you are saying is pretty incredible. I actually think you believe your own story but it's just not possible,' he replied. He turned away at the looks of dejection on their faces. They were nice lads; he didn't like to see them looking so miserable.

Once inside, Alex sat down and placed his head in his hands – Ben and Tom patted him on the back. He'd run out of ideas and didn't know what to think or do next.

Father Williams made them all dinner and left them alone until bedtime. He could tell they were exhausted and very troubled and wished he had an answer to all of this. Alex was still trying to weigh it all up. His thoughts were all over the place and he couldn't make sense of anything. Eventually, he fell asleep.

He was the first to wake the following morning. Father had made breakfast and suggested they spend the rest of the day reading. They didn't feel like arguing and so obediently went into a room where there was an extensive library.

Ben slumped into a chair and put his head on the table with his arms wrapped around his head. Although he made no sound Alex could see his shoulders shaking and knew that he was crying. This was so unlike Ben – he was normally quite unflappable. Tom was the one who would get upset at the least little thing. Alex knew that he would be embarrassed but went over and placed a hand on his shoulder. Ben lifted his head and wiped his eyes with the back of his sleeve.

'Just tired,' he sniffed, 'and homesick…d'you know, I miss my little brother most of all. He can be the biggest pain in the world, but I still want to see him again.'

Alex jumped up so suddenly and whooped that Ben blinked and Tom rounded on him.

'What the heck is up with you? Have you totally lost it?'

Alex was jumping up and down and waving his hands in the air. He slapped one hand on his forehead whilst his friends gawped at him.

'Why on earth didn't we think of this before?' he exclaimed. 'CHARLIE!'

'Yes…and?' said Tom, slowly.

'Charlie! Little Charlie! He will probably still be alive!' Alex yelled.

'Flippin' heck, of course,' said Ben. 'He'll be 65, won't he? We've got to find him!'

Father Williams, who had heard the commotion, put his head around the door and asked what all the excitement was about.

'It's Ben's brother, Father.' Grinned Alex, his eyes alight with this realisation. 'He's probably still alive and if we can find him, he'll prove that we're telling the truth.'

'Well, I can't let you all go off to Keswick on your own. Sergeant Tripp said you have to remain in my care until he traces your parents.'

'Don't you see, he'll never find our parents. They would be in their 90s and as we have said probably dead. Please, Father Williams, we must go to Keswick and find Charlie.'

The boys looked up hopefully at Father Williams. 'Well, I don't know,' he said sighing. 'I'm getting too old to be chasing around and I don't want to get on the wrong side of the law.' What he wasn't saying was that he didn't want to be chasing around on a wild goose chase.

Ben sniffed again and wiped his face with an already damp sleeve. Father Williams handed him a tissue from a box on the table.

'Oh, all right,' he said gently. 'I don't suppose it will do any harm, after all, Sergeant Tripp did only say I shouldn't let you out of my sight.'

Alex could sense though, that he'd only agreed in order to pacify them.

"Can we go now?" Asked Ben looking a lot happier.

"Well, I suppose we could go today – there are no services on a Saturday – we haven't had a wedding for some time and there has been no christenings, either."

The boys were in cheerful moods while they all got ready – Alex's mind was in a whirl. What if Charlie had moved away – what if he didn't remember them – he'd only been five when they were taken. Worse still – what if he had died too. He hoped that he had not given his friends false hope. It was with mixed feelings that he put his coat around his shoulders and walked out to the car with his friends.

Alex could guess that Father Williams wanted to get this trip over with as soon as possible. He'd want to put an end to their fantastical story. He smiled to himself – wouldn't he get a shock when they found Charlie. Well… if they found him…Alex shivered and kept his thoughts to himself.

They set off in Father William's car – it was nothing like they had seen before. It was a small red vehicle with a number of small screens on the dashboard. They all watched in astonishment as Father William's spoke instructions into a small microphone – it thanked him politely before the car started up and set off down the road.

"Cool!" said Alex," How does it do that?"

Father Williams gave him an odd look but explained that the car's satellite navigation was voice-controlled so it couldn't be stolen. It could also steer clear of traffic hold-ups, diversions, and so on. The car was also computerised so that it started once activated – there was no key to start the ignition and there was no need to lock the car as only his voice could start the engine.

'What are those pictures?' asked Alex. 'Aren't they distracting?'

'No lad, they're just icons. They show me that my parishioners are okay and online. It's something they sign up for.' He smiled. 'It's not in the least distracting...after all, I'm not exactly driving the car, the computer is.'

Alex gazed out of the window, noting all the changes to the scenery, trying not to think too hard about what or who they'd find when they got to Keswick. He couldn't resist a little smile as he imagined the look on Sergeant Tripp's face when they proved him wrong – fingers crossed. Oh, how he prayed they could prove him wrong.

Father Williams did find it hard to believe their story it sounded unreal, although the boys did not come across as liars or pranksters – it was a complete puzzle. He did think that Sergeant Tripp could have actually looked more deeply into their story instead of simply dismissing it as a load of old rubbish.

When they arrived in Keswick it was late morning. The first thing that Alex noted was that the Twa Dogs Inn had been converted to a house, their regular newsagent was now a toy shop, and the hall which had housed the tourist information was now a small guest house. Worst of all, the bakery was now an electrical store. Alex had loved that shop – it sold the most delicious pastries and cakes. Tom and he would often buy a snack from there if they were in the town centre. Once past the shops, Father Williams directed the car to Ingleby Farm where Ben lived.

Alex knocked on the front door of the farmhouse − the boys stood nervously. They weren't sure who would answer, or what they would say. After a few moments, a young woman, who Alex guessed to be in her 30s opened the door. Two toddlers hung onto her skirt, peeping around her to see who they were.

'Sorry to trouble you,' stammered Alex, 'but we wondered if you knew where Charlie Johnson is. He used to live here.'

'Charlie Johnson?'

'Um…he's a relative of mine,' answered Ben crossing his fingers behind his back. He hoped she could remember him.

'Don't know about a Charlie Johnson…although we bought the farm about ten years ago from a Mr and Mrs Johnson. They were moving into sheltered accommodation" The Lonsdale" in Keswick,' she said, 'hang on, I can find the address for you.'

'Charlie was their son,' Ben offered by way of explanation.

'I'm really sorry, I don't know him,' she said, handing a piece of paper to him. 'That's the address anyway. I hope you find him.'

They thanked the lady for her time. It looked as though she had very little time on her hands as it was. They got back in Father Williams's car. Ben could hardly hide his excitement at the thought of seeing his mum and dad again − ten years was an awfully long time though, and his stomach churned with a mixture of hope and fear. At least if they found his parents, they could prove their story.

Father Williams gave fresh instructions to the car and it moved off smoothly – no one spoke during the journey. Father Williams seemed to be going along with the whole scenario, but Alex sensed he still had his doubts about them.

The warden of the sheltered accommodation, a homely-looking woman dressed in a neat pale grey uniform opened the door to them. She looked about 50 or thereabouts to Alex – he had a weird thought that if this was the case, he would have been born 20 years before her.

This time it was Ben's turn to speak first. He told the woman that they were hoping to see his parents, Mr and Mrs Johnson. The look on her face told them the answer – Ben bowed his head and two tears rolled down his cheeks – he turned away. The warden's eyes narrowed.

'I'm sorry, but you can't possibly be their son,' she said. Alex reacted swiftly.

'It's a long story...but they are his parents,' he said.

'Well...' she said, softening slightly. 'I'm really sorry to have to tell you that they are no longer with us. They passed away within a few days of each other around, oh, five or six years ago. I'm really sorry, son...' She reached out a hand to touch Ben's shoulder. 'It was so sad, a lovely couple they were, never quite got over losing Charlie's older brother, Ben, I think it was...he disappeared, along with two other boys from the area. It will be about 60 years ago, now.'

Ben whirled around to look at her, then at Father Williams, who was staring at the woman with his mouth open. The reality of what she had just said had struck the father speechless. Alex was quick to respond.

'Do you know where Charlie lives? We really need to find him.'

The warden turned her attention to Father Williams. 'I don't understand this but perhaps you can explain,' she said, her hands on her hips.

'As the lad said, it's a long story but I can assure you, that they are speaking the truth, although, I must admit, I didn't believe them at first.' He smiled as he proffered his identity card, assuming that she would need this before giving out any personal details. She took it and examined it closely – she'd already given out too much information and was feeling slightly guilty. She looked up.

'He used to live on the outskirts of Keswick,' she said, handing the card back to Father Williams, 'he taught at one of the local primary schools, as far as I can remember. I'll have a look on the records for his address.' She turned and disappeared through a door at the other end of the hall. A couple of minutes later, she handed a computer printout to Father Williams. 'I don't know if he still lives there, it's been around five years since…you know.'

They all thanked her and left. She wished them luck as she shut the door shaking her head as she went back inside. She knew that some women were having children later in life, but surely this was a bit too unbelievable…the boys had all seemed nice and polite and Father Williams, a sensible man, *oh never mind*, she muttered to herself.

As they got back into the car Alex noticed that Father Williams was staring blankly through the windscreen.

'Are you okay?' he asked.

'Yes.' He sighed. 'I'm just shocked at what I've just heard, that's all. I'm getting too old to understand mysteries, as this one seems to be. What you have been telling me seems absolutely incredible, but there is obviously something in it. I would like to get to the bottom of this as much as you do.'

He gave directions to the car again, and this time the boys were sat on the edges of their seats with uncontrollable excitement. Within a few minutes, they had arrived at a detached house with a large front garden. A young woman answered the door with a baby in her arms.

Alex wondered if this was perhaps Charlie's daughter or daughter-in-law and grandchild.

'Sorry to bother you but do you know Charlie Johnson, we were given this address for him,' he said, crossing his fingers.

'Yes, we bought this house four years ago from him and his wife but I don't have a forwarding address for them, sorry.'

Alex thanked her and they turned back up the path, his head low.

None of them spoke as they got back into the car but Alex was thinking hard. What were they going to do now? He'd felt hopeful a few minutes ago that they were getting close to finding Charlie.

'It's useless, we're never going to find him now,' Tom said despairingly.

'We will,' Alex said with a sudden determination in his voice. He was remembering what the warden had told them.

'The warden said he was working in a primary school in Keswick. We could contact all the schools, in the area, to find out where he teaches.'

Father Williams explained that although the Education Department would know who worked in which school, they were closed on Saturdays.

However, all was not lost. He could find out the information on the car's computer. All he had to do was swipe his identity card and voila! It might take a while, though, he warned.

Alex sighed impatiently. This was taking longer than he thought and they still didn't know if Charlie was actually still alive or whether he was still working, surely, he was retired by now.

'Here we go!' said Father Williams, after what seemed only a matter of minutes. 'Half a dozen primary schools with a Mr C. Johnson listed at four of them.'

'Oh…we'll just have to visit all of them,' said Alex. 'Oh, it's Saturday.'

'No problem,' said Father Williams, 'there's always someone in schools nowadays even if the children aren't there…however, and I think we should go and get something to eat before we do anything else, I'm a little peckish.'

The boys agreed rather reluctantly − although their stomachs were a little empty − food wasn't at the top of their list of priorities at the present time. They called at a small café, choosing a light meal of sandwiches and pop, which they ate in a hurry, conscious of the need to visit the schools as soon as possible.

It was now mid-afternoon and they had had no luck at three of the schools, The C. Johnsons who taught at them were much younger people. The fourth school, Greenside Primary, was the largest of the schools they had visited. The door led to a large entrance hall with a red-carpeted floor – the walls were full of brightly coloured paintings.

Once the receptionist had examined the vicar's identity card, she confirmed that Charlie Johnson had taught at the school but he had retired six months earlier. She looked at the boys and smiled.

'Grandchildren are you?' she asked, although thinking they did not resemble each other at all.

'He's my uncle,' said Ben. He knew it would be useless to try and explain further.

'Um…do you have his address?' asked Alex.

'I'm sorry, I'm not allowed to divulge that information. Security sanctions…you know the drift.'

Father Williams stepped forward. 'It's imperative that this boy finds his uncle, can't you help at all?'

The receptionist frowned slightly while peering at Ben who she noticed was looking very tense and close to tears. She raised a finger and put it to her lips.

Without another word, she swivelled the computer screen around so that they could see Charlie's address. Father Williams gave her a broad grin and the four of them turned back to the car.

'You might as well sit back and enjoy the ride, lads. It's in Ambleside, over half an hour away.'

As the little car sped along, they all trembled with excitement. After what seemed like an age, they pulled up outside a little bungalow on the brow of a small hill. The paintwork was peeling a little, and the tiles on the doorstep were slightly chipped. Ben knocked on the door and stepped back to wait, flanked by his friends and Father Williams.

A few moments later, it creaked open and a man peered through the gap. His hair was peppered with grey, and he had a bushy moustache. Ben recognised his eyes in an instant and stared.

'Charlie! Charlie! It's me, Ben!'

The man swayed slightly and put his hand on the door jamb. 'I'm sorry…am I supposed to know you?' he asked.

Ben took a deep breath. 'You know me, of course, you know me. But…you might not remember me. I'm your brother, Ben.'

Taking a firmer hold of the door jamb he stared at Ben and then at the others.

'No, lad! You can't be. Ben disappeared a long time ago and he was older than me. Look at you! You must only be about ten or 11.' He began to close the door. 'If this is your idea of a joke, it isn't very funny. Please…just leave me alone.'

'Wait! It is me, honest! Here's Alex and Tom.' Charlie's mouth felt open and he went pale. As he slumped against the wall a woman came hurrying to the door. Glancing at her briefly, he waved an arm at the little group standing outside.

'Are you all right, Charlie?' she asked. He didn't speak but again flicked his hand in the direction of his visitors. Before anyone could say anymore, Alex started to explain what had happened to them, his words coming out in a rush not wishing to be interrupted until he'd finished. Charlie continued to gawp at them until Father Williams interrupted.

'Charlie, Mr Johnson, sir…My name is Father Williams and we have come from St Bees. I still can't fully comprehend the situation but these boys have been very consistent with their story throughout. I have no idea how they came to be at my church but they have tried very hard to find you.'

The woman introduced herself as Charlie's wife and suggested they all come inside. She led Charlie by the hand into the lounge, where he flopped down into an armchair. He still didn't speak. The woman looked at him with obvious concern.

Then Charlie sat up straight and leaned forward. The incredible story Alex had just told him was starting to sink in.

'I don't understand, Lisa. This lad says he's my brother, Ben. You remember, I told you, didn't I? He went missing 60 years ago. Why would someone say something like that, why would they drag up the past?' he said looking utterly confused. As he gazed into the distance it seemed that he was trying desperately to remember something.

'The photographs, where are they, Lisa? The one's in the blue box with Ben's things in it,' he whispered.

Without a word, Lisa got up and left the room. She returned moments later with a blue wooden box. She passed it to Charlie who lifted the lid and frantically searched through the contents. He took out a slightly crumpled photo and showed it to Ben whose face lit up like a beacon.

'That's my old school photo!' he exclaimed. 'See, it is me, Charlie.' Charlie studied the snapshot and then peered at Ben. He got slowly to his feet, dropped the picture and held out his arms. Eyes glistening with tears, he wrapped Ben in a tight hug. He didn't quite understand this but this was his brother. Ben was sobbing, Alex and Tom heaved a huge sigh of relief.

Father Williams and Lisa stood looking stunned. 'I thought I'd never see you again,' Ben said as Charlie finally released him.

Alex was desperate to speak.

'Charlie, we need your help…to come to Whitehaven and speak to the police, they don't believe us. They will have to believe us now,' he said and with that, he turned towards the door.

'Wait!' said Charlie. 'Slow down. This has come as a huge shock. I need to know every little detail of what has happened to you all. I still can't believe what I'm hearing but let's talk and we'll leave first thing in the morning, I promise,' he said beaming at them all. 'You will stay with us too, won't you, Father Williams?'

The evening passed quickly enough and the boys felt a lot more relaxed. Although Charlie and Lisa found it very hard to take in what had happened to the boys, they couldn't deny that this was Ben and his two friends.

They all studied more photos from the box, some of which included Alex and Tom, and they went through the paper cuttings from the time they had all disappeared. It was quite obvious that they were who they claimed to be. Charlie said that their parents had never quite given up on Ben. He recalled how they would argue about whether to stop searching and that his mum would often pack Ben's lunch for school without even thinking about it. Charlie suddenly paused in mid-speech and his face fell.

'Ben, our parents are both dead. I'm so sorry.'

'I know,' he said gently. 'The warden told me.' Then brightened a little.

'Don't forget they are still very much alive, in our time, and they will see me again.'

Charlie patted Ben's shoulder and smiled a little. He'd never been tall enough to do that when they'd both been kids.

'At least they died peacefully,' he added. 'It was within days of each other, both had heart attacks in their sleep, so they wouldn't have known a thing about it.' He looked at Tom and Alex. 'I'm afraid they're all gone now, but as Ben says, not in your" time" . They never got over losing you both.'

They carried on looking at the old pictures and cuttings for a while until Ben spotted a small, faded one showing the young Charlie he knew so well, hand in hand with a little curly-haired girl he didn't recognise.

'Ooh, who's that you're with?' he asked. 'I don't remember her.'

'That's Lisa,' he grinned. 'My Lisa, met her at school just after you lot went missing.'

He showed them a cutting of a newspaper story about their wedding, *'Childhood sweethearts wed,'* said the heading.

'Crumbs!' Ben said, with a grin. 'Some papers will print anything, won't they?

The boys went to bed fairly early, exhausted but very relieved.

'D'you know what?' whispered Alex as they snuggled under the blankets. 'I can't wait to see Sergeant Tripp; he's going to have some apologising to do.' They all laughed.

Chapter 8
A Wasted Journey

Sergeant Tripp had called at the rectory on Saturday lunchtime but of course, there was no reply. He tried later on, again with no luck, and so found himself having to make enquiries around the village. The prospect of trekking around in search of three impudent boys irritated him enormously. The post office was one of his first stops – Mrs Grey usually knew everything that was going on. She wasted no time in telling him that she'd seen Father Williams and his nephews leave in his car, that morning. The Sergeant had neither the will nor the time to put her right on that one, so he simply thanked her and left. Surely, she should've realised that they couldn't be related – they didn't look remotely like each other.

'Something wrong?' she called after him.

'No! What makes you think there might be?' *Nosy old biddy,* he thought.

'Well,' she said, pleased that she'd got his attention. 'First, they turn up out of the blue, and then we see those same three boys' photographs on the news today trying to trace their parents, it said.'

For a minute or so Sergeant Tripp was lost for words. He really didn't want to start explaining things. Mrs Grey would spread the news all around the village and before long the story would be nothing like the truth.

'No,' he said carefully. 'They're just in his care at the minute. Nothing for you to worry about, Mrs Grey.'

When she opened her mouth to ask another question, he cut her short.

'I'm sorry, Mrs Grey, but I really must be off. Thank you so much for your help.' He left, feeling that his sarcasm had probably gone right over her head.

Back at the station, he puzzled over what Father Williams might be up to. Where had be taken those boys? Surely, they hadn't gone back to the Institute…he took his phone out of his pocket.

'Hello, Miss Blackwood, you haven't been bothered by those boys again, have you?'

'No, sergeant, we haven't seen them since you took them back to St Bees. Is there something wrong?'

'No! It seems Father Williams has taken them off on a trip somewhere. Don't worry, I'm sure everything is fine.'

Sergeant Tripp was, in fact, just putting off the moment when he would have to admit to his superior that he had managed to lose three children – for the time being anyway.

Detective Inspector Broom, was, as predicted, not very pleased.

'How stupid are we going to look when these kids' parents come forward?' he spat. 'If we don't find them soon, we, or at least you, are in so much trouble.' Broom drew himself up to his full height.

'So, where do you think they might have gone, Sergeant? On a day trip?' His mouth twitched slightly at the comer, and

Sergeant Tripp could see that his superior was almost enjoying himself.

'I can only think that they have made their way to Keswick, sir...but if they have, I'm really surprised that Father Williams has taken them.'

'Did you visit all of their homes the other day? A matter of course I would have assumed.'

Sergeant Tripp winced. 'Well, no, just Rook Farm and the lady there didn't know anything about Alex's parents.'

'Heavens, man, you should have made further enquiries and gone to the homes of the other two boys.'

Sergeant Tripp didn't answer. He hadn't believed the boys, thought it a complete waste of his time to enquire further but wasn't about to admit this to his superior.

'Well! Don't just stand there, Tripp! Get yourself over to Keswick and do some more investigating, properly this time,' he roared.

It was getting later and all he wanted to do was go home to his wife and two girls. They'd planned a night out with friends and now he had to phone and ask Sandra to delay things. He wasn't looking forward to an excursion to Keswick – he hadn't dared admit to Broom that he didn't even know where Tom or Ben lived or at least, used to live.

Once in Keswick, he started by asking at one of the supermarkets, but none of the staff recognised the photos of the boys. He then called the police station and asked them whether there had been any recent enquiries about the boys, but again there was no record of them. He gave his fellow officers some details, leaving out their story of living in the past and of course the fact that he'd only done half a job himself.

With the help of a couple of bored officers, he visited anything that was still open, but to no avail. No one recognised the boys. As it was getting quite late and he was hungry, he decided to make enquiries at a local pub. He reckoned he could chat with the locals and have a hot meal while he was doing this. He called Sandra again, telling her that he was out in the cold and dark, searching fruitlessly for three lost boys. She was very understanding, but not exactly pleased at having to cancel their arrangements. She asked if she should have a meal ready for him – the girls were already tucking into their dinner – but he declined, saying she wasn't to worry and he would get something to eat in Keswick.

Meanwhile, the mouth-watering smell of fish and chips was calling to him. He wasted no time in entering the pub and ordering his meal.

After he'd eaten, he approached a small group of elderly men playing cards in the comer of the room.

'Any of you recognise these boys?' he asked, rather abruptly, placing the photos on the table amongst their cards.

'That one' – pointing his finger at the one of Ben – 'looks familiar but I can't say from where,' one of the men said.

'Try and think. I need to find these boys.'

Examining the photograph took some time, he was becoming quite impatient and tapped his foot on the floor waiting while they muttered to each other.

'Looks a bit like Charlie Johnson did when he was young, you know the one who was a teacher,' the man who had spoken first said to his colleagues, not looking at the Sergeant. Then there were some 'urns' and 'aahs', until Sergeant Tripp interrupted, becoming increasingly frustrated with them.

'Right! Where do I find this Charlie Johnson, then?'

'Oh, I don't know, not seen him for years now, used to live out at Ingleby Farm years ago.'

'Where's Ingleby Farm?' he asked, shuffling his feet, this was taking far too long. The old man refused to be rushed, finally giving his directions to the farm. Sergeant Tripp left without offering a simple courteous 'thank-you'.

'Why didn't you tell him it was no use trailing all the way over there, they won't know where he is?' one of the other men asked.

'With a rude attitude like that, I didn't feel like helping him,' he sniffed and picked up his beer. 'Let him find out for himself, I say.' And they all laughed and continued with their game of cards.

Sergeant Tripp visited Ingleby Farm where what the boys and Father Williams had been told was repeated. *So...Father Williams is helping them,* he thought.

Surely, he didn't believe their story.

By this time, it was getting late and he felt too tired to make further enquiries. He'd go to the sheltered housing place in the morning but expected it to be another waste of time. He booked into a small hotel and phoned his wife to let her know he wouldn't be home that night.

'Seeing as they've made me come up here and work overtime, they can pay for a night's accommodation,' he told her. He hadn't wanted to but thought it would be wise to let the inspector know what was happening.

The next morning, he had a leisurely breakfast. He was fed up with the whole business and was convinced that traipsing up to the sheltered housing accommodation would be a useless exercise. Johnson was a common name. It was probably a coincidence that the couple had the same surname as Ben. He wasn't honestly bothered whether he found them or not. Those kids were more trouble than they were worth. It was without much expectation that he showed the warden the photographs – she recognised them immediately.

'Oh, yes! They were here yesterday with Father Williams.'

'What did they want?'

'They were after the brother of one of them, that boy,' she said pointing at Ben's photo. 'I must admit, though, it did seem strange that a boy that young could be the brother of a man who is about 60 but—'

Sergeant Tripp interrupted before she had finished. 'Give me the address,' he demanded and gave a sigh.

The warden did as she had been instructed, not at all impressed with the brusque attitude of this officer. At least those children and the father had been polite, alright she didn't understand this strange situation, but they did have good old-fashioned manners.

'As I said to the others, there's no guarantee that he will still be living there. It's over five years since he was last here when his mother and father were still alive.'

Sergeant Tripp left the housing accommodation, barely muttering his thanks. In fact, he was in such a hurry to leave that she didn't get the chance to mention that Charlie had been a teacher in Keswick.

The Sergeant was becoming increasingly irritated. He didn't like wasting energy at the best of times, and this search for the lads was the biggest misuse of his time that he could remember.

He became even more agitated when he called at the address to discover that the owner had absolutely no idea where Charlie lived. She told him the same as she'd told the others.

He returned to his car and absent-mindedly drummed his fingers on the dashboard. The screen sprung to life. Suddenly, he had a brainwave. The Electoral Roll would be online – he typed in a few details. He wasn't at all surprised when page after page of Johnsons came up. There were at least a dozen C. Johnson's too. He sighed, squinted at the helpline number at the top of the screen, and picked up the phone.

Ten minutes later, he was still no further on. It was getting towards lunchtime and already he was thinking of his belly. The civil servant he had spoken to hadn't been very civil at all. She had kept him on hold for what seemed like an age, and then insisted that no, it didn't matter who he was, he would still have to come down to the office, in person, and check the records for himself.

As he drove down there, he passed the pub where he had eaten the night before. He was sorely tempted to go in for lunch, but he didn't want to face those old men again and have to confess that he was still no closer to finding Charlie or the boys. He settled, instead, for a sandwich and a drink from a small bakery.

He wasted another good half hour trawling through dusty paperwork, finding Charlie's last known address and tracing him to Ambleside. He wasn't impressed on arrival, to discover that the house was unoccupied. He saw a curtain twitch at the house next door and decided that he might as well see if he could discover any information from there.

It seemed that Charlie and his wife had left that morning with three boys and a father. Charlie had told his neighbour that they could be away for a few days and had asked her to keep an eye on the house.

'That's how I know,' she sniffed, 'it's not like I'm nosy, or anything.'

Sergeant Tripp was furious. All this time was spent to no avail. *He might as well go back to Whitehaven until they returned,* he thought.

Chapter 9
Proof of Identity

Alex and the others arrived at Whitehaven Police Station late morning. Because Sergeant Tripp was still traipsing around the countryside at that point, they were all shown into Detective Inspector Broom's office. He listened, with interest, to all they had to say – often listening to several voices at once and then leaned back in his chair.

'you say this boy, Ben, is your brother. How do I know that's true? Indeed, how do I know any of these tales about an abduction are true?'

Charlie had already thought of that. He handed the photograph of Ben to the Inspector.

'Yes, that's all very well but you could have had that printed from the photograph in yesterday's paper.'

Alex jumped to his feet.

'No, look at it! It's an old photograph. Tell him, Father Williams,' he begged. He knew he couldn't handle it if the Inspector didn't believe them either.

Father Williams sighed. 'It is true, sir. This gentleman is Ben's brother. I found it very hard to believe myself.' He repeated the conversation they'd had with the warden of the sheltered housing and their search for Charlie. 'They have several photographs of the boys.'

'Okay, this is pretty unbelievable but I'll go along with you for the time being and see where it takes us,' he said and pressed a button on his desk.

'Would you send in a couple of DNA kits, please? I'll need someone to nip them over to the lab, too.'

Alex didn't know what to think. Yes, DNA would prove the link, but surely that would take ages. As if in answer to his silent question, the Inspector nodded at Father Williams.

'Soon have this sorted out, Father. Once we've done the swabs you can all go for a meal in the canteen, the results will only take about 20 minutes.'

Less than half an hour later, they were all assembled back in Inspector's office.

'Well,' said the Inspector. 'I don't know what to say. There is a DNA link to you two,' looking at Charlie and Ben. 'I think it's about time we visited the Institute. No, not you lot, boys, you are all better off staying with Father Williams, if that is alright, Father? We will keep you informed boys.'

Detective Inspector Broom and two constables were leaving the police station when Sergeant Tripp arrived. 'What a wild goose chases I've been on, sir. I found they were visiting Ben's supposed brother in Ambleside, but when I arrived there, they had all left for a couple of days.'

'Yes, I've just seen them, together with Father Williams, Charlie Johnson and his wife.'

'What! They were here?' he exclaimed. 'I hope you reprimanded them severely for wasting police time.'

'No, Tripp. I didn't. We are off to the Institute; you may as well come with us.'

'But…back to the Institute, you can't be serious. Surely you don't believe?'

He was cut off in mid-sentence by the Inspector. 'Don't ask questions and don't make any more assumptions, Tripp. I think you've already done enough harm to this investigation as it is.'

It was the following day, and so far, the boys had heard nothing. Alex was desperate to know what was happening and wondered if Inspector Broom would also be fooled by Miss Blackwood and if their sinister secrets would go undiscovered. Something did cheer him up though – on a walk through the village they saw Sergeant Tripp minus the three stripes on his jacket.

'He's had his sergeant stripes taken off him.' He giggled and they all laughed and waved at him.

When the inspector finally arrived at the rectory later that day, he looked tired and strained. Alex was holding his breath.

'I'm sorry,' he said, 'I'm extremely sorry…' They all stared at him. 'You were right, you were absolutely right. I just can't believe what they've been doing under our noses all this time.'

'Did you find the girls?' Tom asked.

'Yes. When we got there, they were outside helping to carry baskets of vegetables into an outhouse. Miss Blackwood said that the girls were relatives of two of the women. Just visiting, she said. I might have believed her too until I overheard one of the girls asking another woman why her mother was saying that to the police when they lived there.'

'What did you find out?' Charlie asked.

'Well, we've had Miss Blackwood in interrogation since last night and she finally admitted the truth. Those girls were abducted from Ambleside a couple of days before you boys.'

'Oh!' said Alex.

'They used the glass domes you spoke of to extract their memories and then feed in fresh memories of their present life. The technology is only supposed to be used to help Alzheimer's sufferers, but they were set up and used to brainwash those that they kidnapped. Lucky for you three that you escaped.'

'That's terrible,' said Charlie shaking his head. 'That's not the end of it, I'm afraid. Their intentions were to sell the children to women who had lost their own children to the virus.'

'But…I don't understand,' said Alex. 'One of the girls told us that Miss Blackwood was her mother.'

'Yes, that is true which is even more disturbing, when you think, they were going to sell them to someone else,' said the inspector shaking his head. 'Luckily,' he continued, 'they had only taken you three and the two girls so far.'

'What's going to happen to those poor girls?' asked Charlie.

'It's okay, fortunately. The girls have suffered no ill-effects and it will be possible to reverse the procedure. They have been researching the technique for some time.'

'Yes, but I don't understand,' questioned Charlie. 'Wouldn't people be really curious when they saw children turning up when there weren't supposed to be any children in the area?'

'Oh, they had that all worked out,' Inspector Broom replied. 'The children would leave to go to another part of the country with their new parents together, with all the documents they would need to prove that they were related.'

'That is terrible! Those poor children would have been really confused, believing that their mothers whom they had been told were their mothers, had passed them on to new parents!' exclaimed Charlie.

'That was thought about too, all they had to do was provide them with fresh memories of their new parents. Terrible, I agree.' He shook his head and smiled at the boys.

'What's the world coming to? Mind you, it's Miss Blackwood's meticulous paperwork that dropped her in it. We have all the evidence we need.'

Father Williams, who had been quiet throughout, coughed.

'There's no excuse for that cruel kind of behaviour, is there?' he said. 'Although I can understand it, seeing the pain the parents went through on losing their children through the virus, but there is still no excuse.'

'Yes, and the scientists have used the parents' grief to gain financial rewards by selling unfortunate children on to them. I'm afraid the scientists have taken advantage, through the leadership of MissBlackwood and of extensive research into the memory and its dynamics. The women who, tragic as it was, lost their children to the virus would not have chosen to enquire where these children came from.'

With the stunning news that they could have ended up with their identities lost forever, Alex had almost forgotten about getting home to their own time.

Detective Broom interrupted his thoughts.

'We've taken all the scientists and the men into custody and the matter will go to court in the next day or so,' he said

'Hang on!' he suddenly said. 'What men?'

Inspector Broom laughed. 'The" browns" as you called them were men who worked there during the day. They all have homes in Whitehaven and it was them, although I don't know which individual ones that abducted you boys and the girls. Their main jobs were to grow produce which they then sold on to shops and supermarkets in the area.'

'We thought they were perhaps aliens,' he said and they all laughed.

'No, Alex, they are human, and were paid a considerable amount of money to carry out the abductions and keep quiet about the whole operation.'

Chapter 10
Back to Summer

The information that had come to light was absolutely staggering but Alex wondered if the inspector had actually seen the 'time' machine, he hadn't mentioned that. As if he had read the thoughts flashing through his mind, Inspector Broom spoke again.

'Ah, yes, I forgot. The machine you spoke about, I don't know how long they've had that. We knew there had been massive progress made with these transportation machines but I didn't know they had a functioning one. You were right, though, Alex, they could make it invisible and it was in that space you described behind the curtain.'

'So, can we go home, then?' he asked. He'd never felt so happy and almost wanted to launch himself at the Inspector and give him a big hug. Well almost.

'Not yet, I'm afraid. I need you to make statements for the court first." Officer" Tripp and a colleague will escort Miss Blackwood to the Institute in a day or two. You will all be going home soon enough.'

'*Officer*' Tripp, Alex smiled. *So, he has been demoted from his sergeant status, serves him right for not believing us.*

Father Williams, Charlie and Lisa still couldn't fully comprehend what had happened and were amazed to think that they would have got away with their crime, undetected, if the boys hadn't sought out the truth.

Inspector Broom told them all that the boys wouldn't need to sit in court as their video statements would be read out and they would be able to hear what was happening through a video link in another room. He felt they would all be sent to prison for quite a long time.

'Where are the girls now?' Alex asked.

'At the Institute, laddie. We've got them undoing the brainwashing, for want of a better word. Needs a lot of care. Can't be rushed, you know.'

'Oh, that reminds me, Father Williams, I don't suppose you could take the girls in, as well, for a day or so once they are able to leave the Institute, could you?'

'Well, yes, of course. I've got a big enough place here.'

Ben asked if he could go back to Ambleside to spend time with Charlie and Lisa before they returned home to their own time. After all, they had a lot to catch up on. The inspector said that he could see no problem with that and left the Rectory. He still had a pile of paperwork to prepare for the court.

The two girls were brought to the Rectory the next day by the inspector. They all had lots to talk about. Their real names were Dawn and Louise. Dawn was the tall girl and they were both nine years of age, younger than the boys. They had both been taken, as the boys had, from a field near their homes in Ambleside, both at the same time. The scientists had given them medication the first night to help them sleep, then when given tablets the second night, that was the last thing they remembered. Their memories had been replaced without them knowing anything about it. They didn't recall being placed into the glass domes, or anything else about their abduction until their memories had been reversed at the Institute. It has been carefully explained to them what had happened.

The court session was very brief and painless. The boys had simply sat in another room with a video link and listened to all the statements being read out. There weren't really any questions to answer because all the evidence was there and it was undeniable. The men dressed in brown had been cautioned and sentenced to working in the community, continuing with their work in agriculture and would be supervised regularly. The scientists would all serve a lengthy prison sentence and the Institute closed down, until such time that reliable scientists could take over the research, under controlled supervision by the government, and monitored by the police department. They would make sure that nothing like this ever happened again.

The following day, Detective Inspector Broom escorted Father Williams, Alex, Tom and the two girls to the Institute where they were met by Charlie, Lisa and Ben. Miss Blackwood, Officer Tripp and another police officer were already there. Alex noticed, with some satisfaction, that Officer Tripp didn't look very happy. He couldn't resist nodding at him and giving him a smug grin.

All too soon, it was time to say farewell to Charlie, Lisa and Father Williams.

'See you very soon, Charlie,' said Ben laughing as he gave his younger brother a big hug.

'See you in the future, Father. We will remember you and thank you for helping us find out the truth. Without you we would have been lost forever,' said Alex and they all shook his hands and hugged him.

'You're all good boys and it's been a pleasure to help you, even if I didn't believe you at first. I reckon I'll miss you all. Look after yourselves, boys.'

Alex looked at him – he could swear he had tears forming in his eyes.

The five youngsters climbed the steps of the transportation machine – which this time wasn't invisible – followed by Inspector Broom, Officer Tripp, and Miss Blackwood. Inspector Broom was not going to risk Miss Blackwood escaping to another timeline. No, she was going back to 2070 to serve her sentence.

Although Ben was grinning from ear to ear – all the boys were – he could see that Charlie and Lisa had tears in their eyes. Miss Blackwood pressed buttons on the control unit as they strapped themselves in.

There was a loud whooshing and whirring noise inside the machine, an array of tiny, coloured explosions and everything went hazy as they were pinned against the wall of the machine. Moments later or so it seemed, they heard a sucking noise and the machine went silent. They unfastened their straps and stumbled towards the opening door. The steps flopped down to the same pasture he'd been snatched from so swiftly.

Warm fresh air wafted into the capsule as the boys stood and stared. They couldn't quite believe they were home. Dawn broke the silence.

'Is this where you all live, then?'

'Yes,' grinned Alex, 'I do, Tom and Ben live on nearby farms. If you all come to my house, we'll get your parents to come over,' he said, and with that, he flew down the steps. On reaching the ground, he looked up at Officer Tripp.

'You should have believed us, shouldn't you?' And then smiled. 'But…I suppose anyone can make mistakes and it must have sounded strange, though.' He didn't have the heart to be mean to him, he had probably had enough said to him by his inspector.

They were home, the mystery solved and none of that mattered anymore. Officer Tripp didn't acknowledge Alex but he forced a half smile before the door closed. Detective Inspector Broom waved and wished them all well before the machine disappeared.

Chapter 11
Home

Alex couldn't run fast enough back to Rook Farm. The others had trouble keeping up with him, but they all yelled and shouted. Alex spotted his dad on the tractor and staggered over the stubble towards him, screaming over the sound of the engine.

Alex didn't imagine he could have missed his parents so much but now they were within reach he realised how much he had. When his dad finally saw where the noise was coming from, he froze in the seat of the tractor, his eyes wide and staring in disbelief.

Alex had never run so fast. 'Dad! Dad! Dad!' he yelled.

His dad hurled himself off the tractor, and as they reached each other he held him so tight that Alex could hardly get his breath. It was so good to be home.

Hearing the commotion, his mum came out of the house. She looked so tired, but when she saw Alex, she started to sob and held her arms out to her son before slumping to the floor. Alex bent down, brushed the tears from her face and looked into her eyes, his eyes bright with unshed tears.

'It's okay, Mum. I'm home,' he said softly, holding out his hands to help her to her feet. 'And…look here's Tom and

Ben and this is Dawn and Louise.' She started to cry again but this time there was joy on her face.

It turned out to be the most wonderful homecoming. There were huge celebrations amongst all the families of the five missing children. The stories they told were met with astonishment.

His dad had seen him being held by someone, dressed in brown, looking as if he was floating up, away from him, but he hadn't seen any machine.

'Explaining what I saw to your mum and the police was awful, it sounded unbelievable. I told them I'd seen you being raised up into the air by a person, all dressed in brown and then disappearing. Even your mum had difficulty believing me. I even convinced myself, after a while, that it had all been a dream, but it wasn't, was it, son?'

'No Dad, it wasn't,' he said and they all laughed, seeing the funny side of the situation.

Of course, young Charlie didn't understand what had happened. He knew he couldn't find Ben and he'd cried that he'd gone somewhere. And…his mum had cried a lot and his dad had given her a cuddle. He hadn't really understood that his brother had disappeared. Bess stayed very close to Alex for a long time afterwards. The press was full of the story of their mysterious disappearances, and a lot of speculation was made about why no one had been prosecuted for the crime. The youngsters had all been sworn to secrecy and so the rumours circulated for quite some time.

Alex didn't care. They were all home safe with their parents and that was all that mattered.

'You know what, Dad?' he said one day when they were working in the fields, 'I wish you could have met Father

Williams who helped us, but of course, you can't, because he hasn't been born yet,' he said laughing at this, 'but he was a lovely man.'

Alex often thought about the real-life mystery they had been in, and that they had solved it themselves. The boys were determined not to waste the lives that they had so very nearly lost. Alex was to go on to study physics and mechanics. Ben was to go into agricultural and bio-chemical science and Tom concentrated on computer technology. Whilst they had sworn not to change any timeline, they did make one exception.

They wanted to be absolutely sure that no rogue virus was going to kill any children in the future. They had seen the kind of heartache and wouldn't wish it on anyone.

Alex and the others remained good friends with Dawn and Louise. They shared a special bond after what they had all gone through. Sometimes, it seemed as though it had never happened, and they would feel the need to talk about it between themselves.

It was while they were all chatting in Ben's Garden one afternoon when Charlie came trotting across the lawn, holding the hand of a little girl, with blonde, curly hair.

Alex smiled. 'Who's this?' he asked, already guessing what the answer would be.

'It's my friend, Lisa!' exclaimed Charlie. 'She's my bestest friend in the whole world and we're going to get married when we grow up.'

The boys laughed and Alex lay back and gazed at the blue-sky home – it was the best place to be ever. He would never forget their journey to the future but he would never again wish for anything more precious than being 'home' surrounded by family and friends. He sighed, *I wonder if*

Charlie, Father Williams and the other people will remember what happened to three boys and two girls in the future, he thought. He didn't think so but maybe they would have a dream about it all…perhaps when they reached 70 years of age, they could go back to St Bees and visit Father Williams and Inspector Broom – you never knew. When Charlie and Lisa were old enough to understand, they would tell them all about what had happened to them when they were abducted and taken to the future!